MESTER

FOCUS: CARIBBEAN STUDIES

XLI

2012

UNIVERSITY OF CALIFORNIA, LOS ANGELES

Mester (ISSN 0160-2764) is the graduate student journal of the Department of Spanish and Portuguese, University of California, Los Angeles. It is published annually online (http://escholarship.org/uc/ucla_spanport_mester) and in print with the generous assistance of the UCLA Department of Spanish and Portuguese, the Del Amo Foundation, and the UCLA Graduate Students Association.

SUBMISSION GUIDELINES:

To be considered for publication, manuscripts should follow the conventions of the latest edition of the MLA Style Manual. It is presumed that all submissions are original research, and not previously published in any other form. Submissions that are being considered by another journal or any other publisher will not be accepted.

An article submission should have no fewer than 15 pages and no more than 25 double-spaced pages, including endnotes and works cited.

Submissions of reviews for works published within the past year are accepted for the following categories: academic books, linguistics, film and fiction. Reviews should be between 500 and 1500 words in length. Publishers and authors are welcome to submit books for possible selection.

Submissions should be made online at http://escholarship.org/uc/ucla_spanport_mester, where full submission guidelines are posted.

All issues of *Mester* up to Volume 37 are freely available online in their entirety through the Internet Archive at http://www.archive.org/details/mester_journal. Address all correspondence and requests for print copies of issues up to Volume 37 to: Mester, Editor-in-Chief, Department of Spanish and Portuguese, University of California, Los Angeles, Los Angeles, Box 951532, Los Angeles, CA 90095-1532 or mester@ucla.edu. For more information, you may visit http://escholarship.org/uc/ucla_spanport_mester.

For print copies from Volume 38 going forward, purchase Mester through to the link available for that purpose on the issue home page on eScholarship.

Mester is indexed in the MLA International bibliography and is listed in the *ISI Web of Science*.

ISBN 9780983337058

CONTENTS

VOLUME XLI 2012

BOOK REVIEWS

Introduction

We are very proud to present *Mester* XLI, 2012. Two main sections compose this year's volume: one of general interest and a second one that focuses on Caribbean studies and literatures. The original aim of the current volume was to incorporate articles that drew attention to the rich literary and cultural tradition of the Hispanic Caribbean by means of presenting new ideas and critical approaches. However, as our work progressed we realized that, with the exception of Cuba, the Caribbean region—including its continental portion—is still not sufficiently studied. Aesthetic considerations and the restrictions imposed by the cannon seem to be—at least in part—the origin of this lack of representation within the field of literary studies. As a result, an imbalance is constantly created among the Caribbean nations. Conversely, this deficiency also reveals the vast potential that the Caribbean studies offer to scholars and critics. In this context, more attention should be given to the Dominican Republic, a country with an increasing number of residents in the United States and homeland of distinguished writers such as the Pulitzer award winner Junot Díaz.

Hoping to contribute to the revitalization of Caribbean literature, we are pleased to open our volume with an article on the Puerto Rican play *Los soles truncos*. In "The Unwilling Orphan: Trauma and the Decaying Bourgeoisie in *Los soles truncos*," Daniel Arbino approaches the canonical work of René Marqués by way of a theoretical framework that focuses on the trauma caused by the orphanhood of the female characters. He argues that Marqués's orphans function as metaphorical bridges between cultural and personal trauma, allowing the representation of the bourgeoisie as the only victimized group—of the U.S. occupation—despite their history as aggressors. Furthermore, his article asserts that because of trauma the protagonists adhere to a master narrative by favoring an outdated colonial mindset, spreading hate towards other sectors of the population. Arbino's article is followed by two works on Cuban literature. The first of them, "Creating Revolutionary Cuba's National Hero: The Cultural Capital of the *Cimarrón*" by Lindsay Puente, delves into the manners in which radical anti-slavery has been remembered and appropriated into national narratives. Using *Biografía de un cimarrón* as an example, Puente underscores the contradictions that emerge as a result of the efforts of the revolutionary government to incorporate marginal narratives into the construction of Cuba's national identity. In the course of her analysis, Puente affirms that the value of Esteban Montejo's history resides in the fact that it gives voice to alternative forms of resistance without subverting completely the westernized molds of the national hero. The last article of this section focuses on the narratives of the so-called Cuban Special Period. In "La Habana de Antonio José Ponte y Pedro Juan Gutiérrez: el mapa de una ciudad marginal," Damaris Puñales-Alpízar attempts to trace new maps of Havana that have been marginalized from the official history, as well as from the fictional narratives of the nation in the last decades. In her article, Puñales-Alpízar explores how taking as main characters men and women who live outside of the logic of the political discourses, Cuban contemporary narrative underscores the grueling ordeal that constitutes surviving in contemporary Havana. The Caribbean cultures and literatures section closes with an interesting interview with the Cuban writer Pedro Juan Gutiérrez.

Mariška A. Bolyanatz opens the General Section with her article "Ahora, por ejemplo": *ahora* as a discursive deictic in Chilean Spanish." In her article, Bolyanatz provides evidence supporting previous assumptions regarding the changes that the discourse marker *ahora* has undergone, transformations that are related to a process of grammaticalization or subjectification. From Chile we move to Argentina, where Ingrid Norrmann-Vigil conducted research on Porteño Spanish. In the paper "Accounting for Variation of Diminutive Formation in Porteño Spanish," Norrmann-Vigil suggests that although highly productive in Spanish, diminutive formation is not uniform even within a specific dialect. Using a Maximum Entropy Model, her research shows a very significant account for the variation of diminutive formation in the Spanish of Buenos Aires. Closing this section an interview with Rose Mary Salum, founder and director of *Literal: Latin American Voices*, uncovers the challenges of publishing a bilingual and transatlantic literary magazine. Lastly, reviews of the book *La tristeza de los tigres y los misterios de Raúl Ruiz* by Verónica Cortínez and Manfred Engelbert, and the novel *Felicitas Guerrero* by the Argentinean writer Ana María Cabrera accompany our collection of articles and interviews.

I would like to thanks the UCLA Department of Spanish and Portuguese and Stacey Meeker, Director of the Graduate Student Association Publications, for their support. I also would like to express my gratitude to this year's Editorial Board, to our faculty advisors—Jorge Marturano and Ana More—, and to Belén Villarreal for her unconditional help. Being Editor-in-Chief of Mester has been an incredible academic opportunity and an extremely satisfactory experience. We hope that the readers benefit from our work and the articles, interviews and reviews included as part of this volume.

Brenda Ortiz-Loyola
Editor-in-Chief
Mester XLI, 2012

Focus: Caribbean Studies

The Unwilling Orphan: Trauma and the Decaying Bourgeoisie in *Los soles truncos*

Daniel Arbino
University of Minnesota

Throughout literature, orphan protagonists have been a fashionable trope because their absence of genealogical roots frees them from familial obligation and affords them the adventures that intrigue readers as hardships are faced without parental aid and met with a reader's sympathy. At the same time, it is common for orphans, because of their solitude, to want to belong. Through a "forced poetics," a state of desire prevails that provides the orphan with an outlook in which s/he has a certain position and role in a larger national "family."[1] But what happens when society changes and the orphan no longer wants to belong? In this article I argue that orphans who cope with trauma participate in their own alienation and displacement because they eschew societal transformations that directly weaken the colonial class status that they covet. That is, they further divide society since they elect precisely not to belong. *Los soles truncos* (1958) by René Marqués makes use of traumatized orphans of the decaying bourgeoisie in order to criticize what the author perceives to be an oppressive U.S. regime in Puerto Rico through *criollo* protagonist self-victimization and longing for power.[2] I postulate that though the author employs these orphans and their traumatic experiences to show opposition to U.S. occupation, the protagonists also thwart creolizing communities because they favor an outdated European colonial mindset and remain separated from other societal sectors. Afraid to relinquish their privilege, fragmentation prevails because the protagonists are unable to promote racial equality and economic betterment for the largely Afro-Antillean masses. These protagonists are not ambivalent toward the developments transforming their societies but actively resist an era Piotr Sztompka refers to as "the age of change" because of its movements for equal rights, empowerment of the masses, universal education and suffrage (162). Instead, trauma centers on the subjects of a crumbling plantocracy which creates sympathy for them as victims of history, despite their previous role as aggressors and slaveholders.

Los soles truncos is the story of three orphaned sisters living together in a dilapidated house in a post-Spanish-American War society. The sisters are from a wealthy aristocratic and European/*criollo* family whose father owned a sugar hacienda. Through a series of flashbacks, the drama reveals three traumatic moments in which the sisters lost their economic means and class position as a result of a series of misfortunes culminating with the American occupation of Puerto Rico. Their hardships begin with the first traumatic moment: a romance gone awry between Hortensia and the Spanish lieutenant, for whom all three sisters pine. The failed romance causes Hortensia to lock herself in their house and her two sisters never marry either. The next flashback deals with the U.S. invasion of the island and the sisters' subsequent orphaning. The final traumatic moment is the confiscation of their hacienda by the U.S. government, thus forcing the sisters to leave the plantation and move to their urban house. The present finds the sisters living in a decaying house, the last symbol of their opulent past, in Old San Juan having lost their hacienda to pay off part of their debts. Hortensia has recently died of breast cancer. Emilia and Inés continue to try to ward off encroaching debt collectors and foreign investors interested in buying the house and converting it to a small hotel. The drama ends when the sisters, unable and unwilling to change with the times, set fire to the house, burning themselves and Hortensia's corpse as one last stand of resistance against the U.S. occupation.

Los soles truncos is a fruitful text for considering space, time, and social change. In "Los demonios de la duda: el existencialismo en *Los soles truncos* de René Marqués" (2004), Miguel Ángel Náter studies Marqués's use of time and space by demonstrating continuity between the sisters' mindset and their deteriorating house:

> La casa deteriorada y la mente neurótica o esquizofrénica de Inés y Emilia evidentemente manifiestan continuidad. El interior de la casa es el espacio de la eliminación de lo urbano en relación con la nueva modalidad socio-económica; los personajes están instalados, de ese modo, en

el espacio de los hacendados del siglo XIX, mientras el país
ha evolucionado, progresado o retrocedido (94).

According to Náter, the house, a symbol of the Burkhart sisters' own
alienation and opposition to the modernization of the island, must be
burned down with them inside in order for them to escape the absur-
dity of life around them (85). Through an existentialist framework,
Náter effectively shows the powerlessness of humans, in this case
the Burkhart sisters, in front of the change around them. Margarita
Vargas also works with time and transition in her article, "Dreaming
the Nation: Rene Marqués's *Los soles truncos*" (2004). Specifically,
Vargas examines how Marqués uses time to reinforce a patriarchal
colonial society and to denounce a matriarchal commonwealth society
through the "mistrust of women in leadership positions" (42). That
is to say, "during the colonial period the Burkharts represent a semi-
ideal version of the family/nation with the male still as head of the
household, while as a Commonwealth—with the father and mother
no longer present—what is depicted is a grotesque, emasculated resi-
due of a family" that begs for the male figure to continue the nation
(42). In agreement, I evince how these orphan sisters cling to their
colonial past rather than continue nationhood and arrive at a similar
conclusion to that of Vargas: a consequence of Marqués's anti-United
States discourse is that he endows the Burkhart sisters with conserva-
tive ideals about race, gender, and class that they then use to frustrate
a creolizing society.

Perhaps the three most important studies to engage with *Los
soles truncos*, all of which I will return to throughout this article, are
Margot Arce de Vázquez's "*Los soles truncos*: Comedia trágica de
René Marqués" (1979), José Luís González's *El país de cuatro pisos*
(1979) and Juan Gelpí's *Literatura y paternalismo en Puerto Rico*
(1993). Though dated, these three works have presented the foundation with which proceeding studies on *Los soles truncos* (including
my own and the aforementioned articles by Náter and Vargas) dialogue. Arce de Vázquez's article, which appeared in the Puerto Rican
journal *Sin Nombre*'s 1979 special issue on René Marqués, implicitly
refers to trauma as the reason why the Burkhart sisters choose self-
immolation as a sign of victory rather than participating in society.
The author states: "La conducta personal y social de las hermanas
Burkhart ilustra la incapacidad de la clase burguesa dirigente para

reconocer la verdadera naturaleza de la situación política y socio-económica del país y darle la solución adecuada" (58). Their inability to recognize the truth is precisely a result of their traumatic loss of social power due to U.S. occupation coupled with their orphaning. González's seminal text on Puerto Rican identity denounces Marqués's attempt to present the Burkhart sisters as representative of a national identity. González, who postulates that the first Puerto Ricans were of African descent (20), aims to frustrate the identity project posited by Antonio Pedreira in *Insularismo* (1934) and upheld by Marqués that the *criollo* planter, also known as the *jíbaro*, is the symbol of Puerto Rican identity. Therefore, González addresses critical race theory that informs my own work. Gelpí's study bridges generations of yesteryear like Pedreira and Marqués with more recent Puerto Rican writers such as Rosario Ferré, Ana Lydia Vega and Edgardo Rodríguez Juliá by articulating a "crisis del canon" (123). The author examines this "crisis" in depth through the decaying *casa solariega* in *Los soles truncos*. With the destruction of the colonial house, coupled with the death of the paternal figure Papá Burkhart, Gelpí argues that paternalism effectively ended with Marqués's drama, opening up the canon for women and Afro-Puerto Rican writers as well as new modes of cultural expression. The absence of the fatherly figure intersects with my use of the orphan trope, but I engage with how the orphan trope continues colonial patterns.

Whereas the aforementioned authors do acknowledge the colonial mentality of the Burkhart sisters, none of them incorporate a framework of trauma to understand precisely why these girls maintain their Europeanness. As I articulate below, Gelpí and Arce de Vázquez do allude to trauma in the work. However, I am particularly interested in how race, gender, and class intersect as a result of trauma. Such a framework articulates how Marqués conflates personal trauma (orphaning) and cultural trauma (U.S. occupation) to reaffirm his nostalgia for Spanish colonial rule and just as important, an agricultural society. What is more, only González enters into a discussion of race, but stops before acknowledging the importance of the Afro-Puerto Rican *yerbatera* in the drama. This voiceless and nameless figure that ends Hortensia's engagement to the Spanish lieutenant by giving birth to his child is emblematic of a racially creolizing society to which the Burkhart sisters refuse to belong. Through her I discuss how Marqués creates racial tension as the *yerbatera* disrupts a harmonious relationship that would reinforce the Burkharts connection to Europe. To that end, their self-immolation is not a catharsis as Tamara Holzapfel interprets it (155), but rather an affirmation of a colonial mindset highlighting Whiteness and Europeanness that the sisters would rather die to maintain than attempt to integrate themselves into a new society. Finally, I also introduce the orphan trope as a way to think about identity: specifically how orphans who no longer have an affiliation to their colonial past continue to still uphold it and frustrate *mestizaje* in the process.

Orphanhood and trauma are a likely pairing. Piotr Sztompka defines changes as potentially traumatogenic when they are sudden, comprehensive, fundamental, and unexpected (159). Orphanhood, without necessarily having to, fits within all four of these traits. In the case of *Los soles truncos*, the parents' deaths are sudden and unexpected, a result of U.S. occupation. Additionally, orphanhood is comprehensive because it affects all facets of the person's life; it changes memberships in groups, life standards and patterns, social relations and, particularly for single women in a colonial society, economic stability. To that end, it is a fundamental change in that the orphan's world is forever altered for she is no longer able to rely on her parents for financial or moral support. As a result, the women in the text feel unprepared and abandoned, unable to cope with the larger societal changes around them. The trauma adversely affects the mood of the women characters: they become pessimistic regarding the future while nostalgic about the past. In *Los soles truncos* the Burkhart sisters lock themselves inside their house, resigned and helpless. The traumas occur not only on a personal level in the drama, but also on a cultural level. Indeed, the social and racial situations of these characters intersect with their roles as sisters, daughters, and women who are courted and abandoned. When I use the term personal trauma, I refer to Cathy Caruth's widely accepted definition of "a response, sometimes delayed, to an overwhelming event or set of events, which take the form of repeated, intrusive hallucinations, dreams, thoughts or behaviors stemming from the event . . . [T]he event is not assimilated or experienced fully at the time, but only belatedly in its repeated *possession* of the one who experiences it" (*Trauma* 4-5). Thus flashback is prevalent in Marqués's play as the women re-experience events. On a larger scale, cultural trauma happens "when members of a collectivity feel they have been subjected to a horrendous event that leaves indelible marks upon their group consciousness, marking their memories forever and changing their future identity in fundamental and irrevocable ways" (Alexander 1). The collectivity in *Los soles truncos* refers to the decaying bourgeoisie that remains apart from society even though resistance to U.S. intervention could effectively unify. In place of solidarity, the bourgeoisie opts to victimize themselves. This further fragments society in the process.[3] I say that it divides society because the bourgeoisie refuses to recognize the existence of others' trauma and thus negate its responsibility in the affliction of other classes. They leave others to suffer alone as they restrict solidarity (Alexander 1). Furthermore, in order to cope, affected people respond to trauma with various reactions. To be certain, Robert Merton describes a typology of five typical post-traumatic adaptations: conformity, innovation, rebellion, ritualism, and retreatism (139-50). For the purpose of *Los soles truncos* our focus will pertain to ritualism, turning (or rather returning) to established traditions and routines, and cultivating them as safe hideouts to deflect cultural trauma (Sztompka 168). In so doing, the orphan protagonists in Marqués's work halt creolization, or the fusing of heterogeneous characteristics.

Trauma drives the self-destruction of upper class *criolla* women which in turn mark them as counterproductive to building a national consciousness. In *Orphan Narratives* (2007), Valérie Loichot claims that "orphan characters . . . create and master their family narratives . . . An 'orphan narrative' is thus not only a narrative without a parent but, more important, a narrative initiated by the orphan . . . that challenges the master or master-text"(3). Yet because of the multiple traumas that take place, the orphans do not challenge a master-text. That is to say, they are too traumatized to break from the paternalism, linearity, and atavistic genealogy that characterize colonial society. In fact, they aim to maintain it as a vestige of their past. This reinforces a nostalgic yearning for origin, both colonial and familial, in order to make sense of the shift in power that takes place around the orphan sisters. Such desire goes against George Handley's "poetics of oblivion" in which he argues that authors of postplantation societies build upon an acknowledged lack of root. Therefore, counter to Loichot's hypothesis then is that family and colonial constructions win over transforming communities so that definitions of race and colonial mentalities are upheld. The dissolution of colonial power means that solitude and isolation, instead of community, becomes the primary reference for the subject which leads to or reaffirms a weakening of community. This is played out through the trauma that haunts these women. A destabilizing force, trauma is helpful to understand why orphans are not necessarily embracing the rootlessness afforded to them and creating their own narratives. It provides a lens to contest these women characters as resistant orphans who fight against usurpers for the betterment of the "imagined community."[4] On the other hand, when combined with trauma orphan narratives further splinter society because they reinforce the master-texts from which they would otherwise break. The individual subject, failing to process her loss and abandonment, becomes too entrenched in not belonging to identify with a larger community. Therefore trauma becomes exclusive as "something that cannot be denied and that which cannot be confirmed. Whatever pain achieves, it achieves in part through its unsharability" (Scarry 4).

CLASS TRAUMA

"Trauma reveals the limitations of historical as well as psychological truth, in part, by blurring the lines between official histories and individual experiences, between external events and internal reactions to them" (Russ 121). The Burkhart sisters experience a double orphaning in that both parents die in addition to a metaphorical orphaning from their Europeanness. Thus it can be difficult to distinguish personal from cultural traumas as the two are inextricably linked in *Los soles truncos*. This is particularly noteworthy because it connects the plantocracy to the nation; ostensibly one and the same since much of the plantocracy's trauma, as they interpret it, happens because of the insular society's foreign occupation. This is evident in *Los soles truncos* when Papá Burkhart blames the United States for his wife's death: "El dolor de ver flotar una bandera extraña donde siempre flotara su pendón de rojo y gualda. 'De eso muere vuestra mamá, niñas'" (53). When Papá Burkhart blames the United States, he connects two traumas. The wane of bourgeois power after U.S. intervention (a cultural trauma) alongside the rupture of a previously united and well-to-do family (a personal trauma) evinces that Marqués is manipulating the U.S. occupation of their islands to fuse together loss, melancholia, and racial hatred with personal stories of dispossession and displacement. Considering Antonio Benítez Rojo's statement that "hay que concluir que la historiografía del Caribe, en general, se lee como un largo e incongruente relato de legitimación del plantador blanco . . ." (294), one notices that the ill effects of this orphaning continue a process of legitimizing the planter within the nation through parallel occurrences. That is to say, as the plantocracy suffers, so does the nation. This in turn neglects other cultures' contributions to society. Since no historical event *necessarily* qualifies in itself as a cultural trauma (Smelser 35), and since cultural traumas are historically constructed (Smelser 37), it follows that this sentiment of loss and abandonment is not a comprehensive cultural trauma that affects all insular groups equally. On the other hand, the traumas present in this text effectively overlook the traumas of the Afro-Antillean sectors that served as the workforce for the plantocracy's rise to power. Furthermore, the traumas do not consider how U.S. occupation and urban Black Nationalist movements benefit these sectors.

Marqués is regarded as one of Puerto Rico's key playwrights of the twentieth century. Also a novelist and essayist, he often combines political and psychological themes (Cypress 241). Although he staunchly rejected U.S. occupation in favor of independence, in *Los soles truncos* Marqués reveals that nostalgia for Spanish rule shrouded his pro-independence beliefs. Biographically speaking, Marqués is a descendant of the lighter-skinned land-owners in Puerto Rico which influences the trauma their characters experience.[5] He came to be one of the most prominent authors of "La generación del cincuenta" but as Arce de Vásquez points out, Marqués is also a continuation of "La generación del treinta," the children of *ex-hacendados* led by Antonio Pedreira who lauded Spain's paternalistic legacy and denounced both the United States and African elements on the island.[6] Of equal relevance is that Marqués's mentality is comparably outmoded for his generation, which is why he is so often considered alongside Pedreira.[7] That is not to say that other authors of "La generación del cincuenta" are not for independence, but rather that they do not idealize their Spanish heritage in the same way. In his drama *Vejigantes* (1959), which debuted in the same year as *Los soles truncos*, Francisco Arriví offers a divergent perspective through the vindication of African heritage. Ana Lydia Vega and Rosario Ferré, both of later generations, challenge paternalism in their works. Marqués, however, looks back towards Spain as a legacy interrupted traumatically by U.S. occupation. That the Burkhart sisters do not wish to belong stems from this trauma and also reflects Marqués's own pessimism toward U.S. colonialism.

To understand the societal transformations taking place in *Los soles truncos*, one must look at the initial goals of the U.S. regime. In the 1930s, a period that saw the early stages of movement for reform, the educational system in U.S.-controlled Puerto Rico was characterized by three objectives: to Americanize the masses, to impose English, and to make education widespread. The Americans used these objectives to acculturate new colonial subjects, and that era saw an increase of students from previously ineligible sectors of the small- and medium-sized land owners (Rodríguez 88-91). Additionally, life for Afro-Puerto Ricans improved: they were able to influence Puerto Rican life in the twentieth century due to the new democratic and social freedoms that went hand in hand with the political break from Spain, ending a colonial relation which they viewed as synonymous with the plantation society that oppressed and underappreciated them (González 35). Politically, Pedro Albizu Campos, Ernesto Ramos Antonini and José Celso Barbosa, three notable Afro-Puerto Ricans, occupied a variety of posts, ranging from representative of sugar cane workers and pro-independence movements (Albizu Campos) and President of the House of Representatives of Puerto Rico (Ramos Antonini) to U.S. Senator and annexationist (Celso Barbosa). Culturally, Afro-Puerto Rican music genres such as the *plena*, *danza* and *bomba* were more accepted among citizens, though not without detractors (Zenon Cruz 118-121, 295-7). By 1958, the moment of the drama's setting, Puerto Rico had undergone significant industrialization and urbanization. In order to stimulate economic development beginning in the mid-1940s, *Operación Manos a la Obra* encouraged industrialization dependent on privatized U.S. capital (Baldrich 250). As the U.S. took over the island, the privileges that the plantocracy enjoyed and the divisions that Spanish colonialism maintained had ended, but other sectors benefited from improved standards of living. It is because of these developments that one is able to posit that the *criollo* trauma was not universal on the island.

THE RACIAL TRAUMA OF EUROPEANNESS

In *Los soles truncos* the protagonists are characterized by what Curaçaoan writer Frank Martinus Arion terms Europeanness, that is, the tendency of those of European descent to see themselves as superior members of Caribbean society (450). For the Burkhart sisters, the realization that their Europeanness is no longer relevant, whether due to U.S. occupation or rising Afro-Antillean sectors, yields a traumatic experience of loss, rejection and the anxiety of not belonging to either an imperial White or Afro-Antillean world.[8] The first traumatic moment in *Los soles truncos* is a failed romance between Hortensia and a nameless Spanish lieutenant, which ends when he fathers a mulatto baby with an Afro-Puerto Rican *yerbatera* (42).[9] Marqués reverses power differentials through the use of the *yerbatera* to produce a victimization of *criollos*. The result creates disjuncture between the *criollo* and Afro-Puerto Rican sectors because the *yerbatera* transgresses racial hierarchies and blocks matrimony. She is the voiceless home wrecker without a side to the story; Hortensia is the traumatized victim unable to overcome the event with whom the spectator empathizes. Were their engagement to come to fruition, the union between Hortensia and the Spanish lieutenant would represent a reinforced link between the Burkhart family and Spain. Their status as elites would also be reaffirmed, as the marriage would be the ideal culmination to her privileged lifestyle that kept her separated from the Afro-Puerto Rican masses (save for the family servant) and provided her a European education. Of German and Spanish descent, Hortensia Burkhart would only add to her European legacy through marriage with a European, as opposed to a *criollo*. That the *yerbatera* interrupts this seemingly destined union makes her the scapegoat for Hortensia's downward spiral. That she is Afro-Puerto Rican generates racial hatred in the drama because Marqués creates her as an antagonist—a foil to Hortensia that the spectator will disdain because she ruins an inevitable relationship.

In fact, racial background is of such importance to the family that prior to their engagement, Papá Burkhart examines the lieutenant's bloodlines to ensure his purity (40). Hortensia remarks that "Ya sé que somos celtíberos por la rama de Málaga. Mas aún, ahora, al yo casarme, tendremos entre nosotros . . ." (39). The rest of the thought, like the lieutenant's specific genealogical background, is never given, however Hortensia's reaction indicates that it is desirable. The first part of the quote focuses on a Celtiberian lineage that subdues any idea that the family might have North African blood. The need to explicitly discern both sides' lineages comes from a colonial fear of non-European genealogies and miscegenation, but in *Los soles truncos*, only the lieutenant's bloodline, ironically, is questioned. While the Burkhart family investigates the lieutenant's lineage, the sisters apply extra makeup to cover "blackish stains" on their cheeks ("Purificación" 12). The lieutenant, the imperial White in this situation, obviously does not seem as concerned with genealogy because he fathers a mulatto baby. This fact suggests two changes: racial purity has become more important to *criollos* than to imperial Whites, which signifies that colonial models remain firmly in place even as their precedents change. Therefore, the *criollos* need to reaffirm their lineage as they constantly try to prove themselves hierarchically equal to imperial Whites, which they are not. Secondly, *criollo* women of the plantocracy are no longer considered superior partners to Afro-Puerto Ricans.[10] Hortensia was originally courted for her racial and social status, neither of which holds value at the end of the play. In fact, the Spanish lieutenant equates Hortensia, who throughout her life distinguishes herself from the popular classes, with the Afro-Puerto Rican *yerbatera*. This process of "indifferentiation" in which "social hierarchies are first transgressed, then abolished" (Girard 136), produces feelings of displacement and dispossession for the *criollo* class. While Afro-Puerto Ricans reconfigure social hierarchies alongside imperial Whites, the sisters adhere to a colonial ethos as they segregate themselves from Afro-Puerto Rican sectors. As racial and economic change envelops the island, their reclusion becomes more pronounced; the sisters do not want an egalitarian society at their own expense.

The Burkhart sisters are so characterized by their Europeanness that it is difficult to align them with Puerto Rico. Their German last name distinguishes them as foreigners on their native island, as does their schooling abroad that alienated them from islanders. As José Luis González points out:

> presentar ese mundo como el mundo de la 'puertorrique-
> ñidad' enfrentado a la 'adulteración' norteamericana,
> constituye no sólo una tergiversación flagrante de la
> realidad histórica, sino además, y ello es lo verdaderamente
> grave, una agresión a la puertorriqueñidad de la masa
> popular cuyos antepasados (en muchos casos cercanos)
> vivieron en ese mundo como esclavos, como arrimados o
> como peones. (34)

To legitimate the crumbling bourgeoisie's trauma, Marqués singles out this individual family, so apart from the rest of society, and makes it seem like the U.S. occupation afflicts all Puerto Ricans in the same way. This enables him to divert the effects that widespread education, political participation, and improved living conditions have on other societal sectors at the same time. The sisters further betray their insular family by privileging their parents' European heritage over their own Caribbeanness. Even as orphans, with the attempt to connect to their native island and with no familial obligations to Europe, they still choose their Europeanness. Therefore, when Hortensia is betrayed by the Spanish lieutenant, it marks a traumatic recognition that White *criolla* and imperial White have two different meanings. As Susan Burrows puts it, the Burkhart sisters are "white but not quite" (29). In addition to the aforementioned reconfiguration of insular social hierarchies, *criollo* trauma becomes doubly reinforced by the betrayal of imperial White Iberians who have stranded the *hacendado* class, a "white-on-white desertion" (Burrows 29). In post-1898 Puerto Rico, where Afro-Puerto Ricans outnumbered *criollos* and connections to Spain were broken, the Burkharts' racial identity is now a sign of past exploitation. The abandonment that takes place reflects an orphaning that leaves the sisters displaced on their own island. U.S. occupation disconnects the Burkharts from family, European culture, and most importantly, financial security now that their place within the imperialist endeavor has ceased to exist. Yet rather than blame the Spanish lieutenant, the Burkhart sisters continue their allegiance to Spain. Therefore, the blame falls largely on the Afro-Puerto Rican *yerbatera* as the sisters forego an opportunity for solidarity, or at the very least, communication between women. They want to be European and thus they cannot reject the Spaniard, but they can no longer attain that ideal, especially if marriage is not an option. Loss, anxiety, resentment and fear of change lead the sisters to remove themselves from society, unwilling to take part in the U.S. occupation.

FEMALE PLACELESSNESS[11]

Up until now I have considered the traumatic wounding that takes place at social and racial levels, but both of these are of course intertwined with the way Marqués's protagonists experience trauma as a matter of gender. Not one of the Burkhart sisters can imagine her life outside the hegemonic norms that deny her subjectivity. This reasserts that they uphold a paternalistic master-text. What is more, societal conventions demand that women of the privileged class "suppress their will, agency, and sexuality to maintain the power and privilege of the men of their families" (O'Connell 175). Here I evoke Joanna O'Connell's study on Rosario Castellanos because Castellanos' bourgeois protagonists are socially comparable to the Burkhart sisters in their gendered experience that comes as a result of their status in society. For the sake of maintaining their upper class appearance, the Burkhart sisters must act according to a prescribed gender performance that is particular to their class, and what is more, constructed by men. That is to say, their desires and realities must be in line with the patriarchal legacy that their (colonial) father left behind—racial segregation, political and financial authority, and a lack of promiscuity—or such desires must be suppressed or concealed. That is why the sisters never engage in new romances so as not to be perceived as promiscuous. What is more, maintaining this appearance is why they continue to wear expensive jewelry despite their economic decline and why they remain isolated from other racial sectors despite a creolizing society. Because they cling to a paternalistic society, the orphan characters fail to articulate an alternative narrative and instead adhere to the master-text. Indeed, by maintaining racial and sexual differences of the plantocracy, the women participate in their own oppression. This oppression manifests itself economically in their orphanage. Since there are no masculine heirs, it is no longer possible to connect the family's genealogy to a time or place. In other words, the root is lost and there is a disappearance of authority that articulates the sisters' vulnerabilities as women. The death of the father, the sole earner in the family, in conjunction with the end of Spanish colonialism, halts the family's prosperity. The lack of financial security displaces *criolla* women from their long-standing class power and Europeanness and leaving them as outcasts on their native island. Armanda Lewis points out that Latin American authors who use female orphans "depict the economic vulnerability of women without husbands, fathers or patrons. Also directly implicated is the nation's lack of preparing all of its citizens for life without a patron" (18).

Though her focus is on nineteenth-century authors and nation, Lewis's insight is applicable to *Los soles truncos*. Doubly orphaned and abruptly cut off from Europe and their father, these women are also unprepared to survive outside of the imperial endeavor. This is because, as Françoise Vergès states, "in the colonial family romance, children remained children forever" (6). That is to say that the Spanish colonial system's longevity was in large part a result of their ability to keep its colonial populace dependent upon the metropole as its *patria*. When Spain left Puerto Rico, it abandoned its role as *patria*. Additionally, the use of female orphans functions as a further critique against U.S. occupation and the rise of Afro-Antillean sectors. The former is responsible for their loss because it ruptures the bourgeoisie's hegemonic power and the latter usurps it. However, their abandonment also reveals a dependency that is gendered in the text. They are vulnerable because they lost their male patrons, characterizing them as dependent female orphans and perpetuating myths of women's inferiority upheld by Marqués. Luce Irigaray notes that "a single subject, traditionally the masculine subject, had constructed the world according to a single perspective" (Hirsch 145), specifically through dichotomous oppositions of Masculine/Feminine, Truth/Error, Independent/Dependent, Being/Nothingness, Self/Other that has allowed masculine discourse to render women subordinate to and dependent on men (Felman 22; Irigaray 197). The result is a patriarchal privileging, or to borrow Derrida's term, phallogocentrism (xxv). Indeed, in the phallogocentric setting of Marqués's drama, these dichotomous hierarchies of inequality play out through the orphaned sisters and the absent male patrons; the (colonial) father.

Once Spanish colonialism ends in *Los soles truncos*, the sisters are left with no parental directive and nothing ever comes to fill in for that paternal absence, neither a husband nor the United States. Since the engagement to the Spanish lieutenant ends abruptly, the sisters have no manner of income save for Inés who begs for money. The death of the father, then, becomes the moment of displacement for the Burkharts. In agreement, Juan Gelpí states:

> De manera significativa, en el Segundo acto de *Los soles truncos* Inés narra cómo se coloca el cadáver de su padre 'en el centro de la sala'. Ese espacio central del escenario se halla, entonces, habitado por la pérdida irrecuperable de la figura paterna y de todo lo que ella representa: el mundo de los hacendados, la estabilidad, y una cierta armonía que, según esta obra, caracterizaba el pasado patriarcal . . . la muerte de Papá Burkhart figura además como un *trauma*

> que lleva a las hermanas Burkhart a una época signada por
> la inestabilidad y la crisis. (124)

The overall trauma here is the rupture of time, and with it the lifestyle the daughters have always enjoyed. "Y el tiempo entonces se partió en dos: atrás quedóse el mundo de la vida segura. Y el presente tornóse en el comienzo de un futuro preñado de desastres. Como si la muerte esta vez hubiese sido el filo atroz de un cuchillo que cercenara el tiempo, y dejase escapar por su herida un torbellino de cosas jamás soñadas" (70). Though they desire to return to what they once had, death and U.S. occupation makes such a return impossible. Thus they inherit a melancholic and pessimistic present whose uncertainty manifests anxiety in the sisters. But the trauma of class is intersected with gender because as power is fought for and negotiated among the United States, the Afro-Puerto Rican and *criollo* sectors, the *criolla* woman fails to gain a stronghold on any meaningful social power (Handley 153). Once wealthy *criollas*, the three women have no manner to financially sustain themselves. They are not prepared to work because their entire lives were provided for. No longer are they among the select few to receive an education and what is more, their education pertains to a domestic space. The sisters are left without a place in the public sector—they are ultimately supposed to marry Spaniards and perpetuate their dependence as housewives,—which is why so much of their melancholia also has to do with Hortensia's failed engagement. Were one of them a man, or were they a family of a lower class, such as the *yerbatera*'s, a similar problem would not occur because a job is customary. The first part of that scenario demonstrates gender differences in a colonial society whereas the second part speaks to racial and class differences. Upper-class *criolla* women are not raised to work outside of the house; they are raised to be homemakers. However, those that do not marry suffer from their portrayal as "old maids" or "spinsters," characterized as resentful, celibate, and apart. The reality is that the sisters no longer have value now that their class status is insignificant. Their inheritance has been squandered which provides little motivation for someone to marry one of them so that without husbands and without means to earn a living, the sisters are displaced in society. They are traumatically abandoned by all forms of patriarchy to fend for themselves and yet they are so shrouded in patriarchy that they do not know how to survive without it. Portraying the women so economically vulnerable further increases the spectator's empathy towards the *criollo* class while highlighting the U.S.'s destructive manner towards them. In the end, however, the Burkharts choose their past relevance over their present means of survival. When the sisters decide to burn themselves inside their house, they adorn themselves with lavish jewels that could have ostensibly been used to pay bills (81). The jewels, like their house, are their link to the past—a time when they had a place in society. Rather than shed that link and forge ahead in a new society, the orphans cling to their colonial dominance through their material possessions.

This experienced loss, coupled with *criolla* placelessness manifests as fatal breast cancer in Hortensia. Certainly the location of the cancer, the breast, which lies above the heart, figuratively speaks to the trauma of her failed romance. Breast cancer also speaks to her gender identity, since, though prevalent in men, it is commonly associated with women. Indeed, the cancer that occupies Hortensia's body evokes ideas of inertia which recall Susan Sontag's argument that ". . . cancer is a disease of insufficient passion, afflicting those who are sexually repressed, *inhibited*, unspontaneous, incapable of expressing anger" (21, my emphasis). I point to inhibited because Hortensia is restrained by the limitations of colonial society that are imposed on *criolla* women. Under the new regime, Hortensia has few choices without renouncing her background. Financially, she is no longer desirable to suitors and therefore, no one ever tries to coerce her out of the house. Indeed, as a woman, Hortensia is preoccupied with the notion of "honor," a societal convention from which men are excused, but which weighs heavily on a woman's reputation particularly in a small insular society. Hortensia's removal from society for fear of shame leads her to a life of sexual repression since she never dates again. Therefore, Hortensia lacks the mores to be a part of the new society since the possibility of public humiliation has been curtailed due to the U.S. occupation's restructuring of classes. On the contrary, U.S. occupation could be seen as a *tabula rasa* for Hortensia's love life as she is no longer bound by colonial hierarchies. Yet unable to process the loss she suffered in the breakup with the Spanish lieutenant, Hortensia remains an abandoned outsider of the new society. She opts to uphold Eurocentric ideals that have marked the *hacendado* class as obsolete. Restricted by her Europeanness, Hortensia never attempts to work or fit in within a changing society. Indeed, her "temporal liminality—belonging to a system that is no longer what it used to be but yet not dead—evokes the unfathomable space of dying" that manifests as breast cancer (Loichot 24).[12] Marqués portrays tragedy among the *hacendado* elites, particularly vulnerable women, to suggest a return to the Spanish rule that he desires.

Coping with Trauma

"Defeatism, quietism and resignation are manifested in escape mechanisms which ultimately lead them to 'escape' from the requirements of society" (Merton 148-9). When coping mechanisms, such as those suggested by Merton, do not work, suicide becomes a last resort for those who cannot deal with the extreme pain—depression, anxiety, helplessness, hopelessness, etc.—(Briere 61). Interestingly, Marqués points out that Puerto Rico has the highest incidence of suicide for Catholic states in the world in the 1950s. He directly attributes this stat to the island's nationalist spirit confronting the harsh reality of occupation ("El puertorriqueño"157). It is therefore relevant to think about the suicide that takes place in *Los soles truncos* as a response to the trauma of the U.S. occupation. Indeed, the invasion of the United States, for the sisters, is an interruption of time, in which modernity imposes itself. Therefore, "time" is constantly referenced in the drama. Emilia, for example, when talking about how their lives have endured hardship talks about "todo lo feo lo ha traído el tiempo" (54), which is an implicit reference to modernity and the U.S. invasion. After all, modernity, along with imperial invasion, weakened cultures through cross-cultural exchange. The U.S. arrival not only kills the Burkhart sisters' parents, but also threatens their culture. Consequently, when the sisters decide to burn themselves alive in *Los soles truncos*, Inés expresses that "por esta vez el tiempo nos pertenece" (80). To view this battle with time as resistant to U.S. occupation, also shows it as resistant to the end of Spanish colonialism in which everyone else seems to be participating—emphasizing the sisters' separation from insular society.

Yet the one remaining refuge in their spatial universe from foreign occupation is their now-dilapidated house in Old San Juan. For instance, the furniture, although deteriorated, shows an opulent past that connected the family to Spain: "una butaca Luis XV," "un sillón de Viena," and "una silla estilo Imperio" all speak to a relationship with Europe, while "un gran mantón de Manila" incorporates Spain's colony in the Pacific (26; 27). These pieces serve as metaphorical sites of both remembrance and loss. On the one hand, their presence reminds the girls of their affluent and happy childhood, constantly recalling positive memories to help them cope with a legacy now lost due to U.S. occupation. Conversely, their depreciated condition mirrors the sisters' present reality. In that sense, every time they see the furniture, the sisters unknowingly re-experience their loss. In agreement, Whitehead states that "one of the key literary strategies in trauma fiction is the device of repetition, which can act at the levels of language, imagery or plot. Repetition mimics the effects of trauma, for it suggests the insistent return of the event and the disruption of narrative chronology or progression" (86). By reliving this historic moment through theatrical performances, Marqués utilizes *Los soles truncos* to remind audiences of the U.S. invasion of the island and the grave effects it had on the *criollo* class. Thus, when the tax collectors show up at their doorstep, Emilia and the spectator cheers on Inés to defend their home and island from U.S. occupation. "Eso es, Inés. Defiende tu casa. La casa de mamá Eugenia. De papá Burkhart. La de la nana negra que nos lloraba, y nos cantaba, y nos mecía, sin oponerse al tiempo. La de Hortensia y Emilia. La casa nuestra" (75). Whether "la casa nuestra" is a metaphor for the old Spanish colony or a more literal understanding of their house, the conclusion remains the same: the sisters link "home" with the nostalgic colonial past as Emilia refers to important people and fond memories of their childhood. Therefore, to defend their house from the encroaching American tax collectors and investors who want to turn it into a luxury hotel is to defend their Spanish values and upbringing.[13] With dealienation impossible, the sisters choose one last act of resistance, burning themselves alive in a house that was a symbol of the past, but cannot be a part of Puerto Rico's new political present. Unable to cope any longer, they choose death over integration.

Conclusion

If nations are bound together not by what they choose to remember, but by what they choose to forget as Ernest Renan suggests, then the insular society in *Los soles truncos* exposes the folly of the concept of modern nation in the Caribbean region.[14] Ideas of harmony, homogeneity and oneness that citizens of a nation are believed to share are noticeably absent. In response to the Francophone Creolists' manifesto *Éloge de la créolité* [*In Praise of Creoleness*] (1989), Arion's "The Great Curassow or the Road to Caribbeanness" (1998) all but concludes the twentieth century with the realization that at the time of writing, Caribbeanness, let alone Creoleness has yet to come to fruition.[15] On the other hand, making note of the segregation in which cultures exist on the Caribbean, Arion declares that "the region as a whole has not even reached the stage of Caribbeanness or even Americanness yet" (448). Arion points to a continued migration to the Caribbean from Europe but a lack of migration from Africa, which in turn diminishes the presence of African cultural elements, such as trickster tales. His point is that Caribbean societies are still largely fragmented and have never homogenized into a national identity. In that sense, creolization is not a workable concept in Caribbean literature because the characters in *Los soles truncos* are still searching for racial exclusivity.[16] The characters do not live up to the ideals proposed by creolization and remain divided by language, race, class, and gender (Malena 5). In the aforementioned article, I have demonstrated that part of this splintering has to do with the plantocracy's consequential trauma from a loss of power (whether due to industrialization and/or foreign occupation), orphaning (loss of family/nation), and the transgression of outmoded racial hierarchies resulting in *criollo* displacement. Orphans specifically are used as metaphorical bridges between cultural and personal trauma. They are a means to engage the reader/spectator on an empathetic level that later expands to a societal level where the decaying bourgeoisie is victimized. The Burkhart sisters are counterproductive because they refuse to accept their loss of power to meet the changes of their insular society. This is emphasized by the solitude in which the Burkhart sisters live. To say nothing of Afro-Antillean trauma that stems from the Middle Passage, slavery, and post-emancipation insular race relations that engage the popular classes, the plantocracy's own traumatic conditions have revealed disjointed sectors sharing an island, but in "complete ignorance of each other's existence" (Arion 449).

Notes

1. By "forced poetics" I refer to Édouard Glissant's definition as a collective situation in which "a need for expression confronts an inability to achieve expression" (120).

2. *Los soles truncos* is based on a short story by Marqués, "Purificación en la Calle del Cristo" (1958). I will refer to the short story when I feel that context is missing from the drama. The term *criollo* refers to children born in the Americas but of Iberian descent.

3. Dominick LaCapra terms 'vicarious victimhood,' whereby one shifts empathy onto him or herself by taking the place of the victim or oppressed (47), which is what the decaying plantocracy does in this work.

4. Benedict Anderson first coined the term "Imagined Communities" in his 1983 text of the same name. Anderson defines an "imagined community" as a group of people who share a common identity united by moral, religious, cultural, and linguistic discourses despite the fact that "[the community] is imagined because the members of even the smallest nation will never know most of their fellow members, meet them, or even hear of them, yet in the minds of each lives the image of their communion" (6). To that end, the nation, according to Anderson, is a social construct.

5. Arcadio Díaz Quiñones points out that Marqués "procedía de una familia de terratenientes, que había pasado su infancia con sus abuelos agricultores, formado por los valores y la visión de mundo de una sociedad agraria, patriarcal y paternalista" (*El almuerzo* 146).

6. Arce de Vázquez comments that Marqués "estaba muy cerca de la ideología de los escritores de la Generación del '30 y, en ciertos aspectos, vino a ser su continuador y transmisor a su propia generación y a la siguiente. Esta situación fronteriza de su pensamiento y obra literaria—lo que acepta y lo que rechaza de sus precursores inmediatos—hay que tenerla muy en cuenta para juzgarla con justicia" (59). José Luis González echoes this sentiment: Marqués "pertenece ideológicamente a la generación del treinta" (*Conversación* 70).

7. Here I refer to a canonical work of Puerto Rican culture studies, Antonio Pedreira, *Insularismo* (1934).

8. I use the term "imperial White" to refer to the Whites native to Europe as opposed to those native to the Antilles.

9. Because of their Europeanness, the three sisters all view the nameless Spanish lieutenant as the ideal man. Although a relationship between him and Hortensia emerges, it is not without competition: the Burkhart sisters' desire to marry a Spaniard eclipses their own loyalty to each other as betrayal is an implicit theme in the work.

10. The fact that the mulatto is public knowledge allows us to deduce that it is not a secretive relationship.

11. I borrow this term from George Handley's study on Jean Rhys's *Wide Sargasso Sea* in which he describes the "placelessness of the Creole woman" as "a criticism of male legal power that also vacillates between a resistance to and nostalgia for empire and a concomitant attraction and repulsion toward Afro-Caribbean culture" (151).

12. Here Loichot refers to William Faulkner and Saint-John Perse. While the first part of this citation is also applicable to the Burkhart sisters, the protagonists differ from the two authors in that the characters do not share the same irreconcilable tension toward the community. According to Loichot, Faulkner and Saint-John Perse "do not politically embrace the oppressor's opinions, yet they are immersed by their social situation, in the plantocracy oppressing another race" (24); the protagonists in *Los soles truncos*, however, do embrace the oppressor's opinions.

13. Although the role of the Afro-Puerto Rican nanny within the declaration gives pause to reconsider the meaning of "our house" as a possible reconstruction of family, that she is reduced to a worker who does not question her role even as the times change speaks to a longing for colonial hierarchies as noted by the nameless, stereotypical Black Nanny persona that dehumanizes her.

14. I refer to the statement that "Forgetfulness, and I shall even say historical error, form an essential factor in the creation of a nation . . ." (166).

15. To be certain, Bernabé, Confiant, and Chamoiseau postulate the culmination of Creoleness. Americanness is the first stage when Western populations in the New World had no real interaction with other cultures. In this case original cultures are adapted to new geographical environments. "*Americanness is therefore, in many respects, a migrant culture* in a splendid isolation" (92). Secondly they define Caribbeanness as being like Americanness but on the Caribbean Archipelago and referring to isolated Asian, European and African communities. Caribbeanness is a geopolitical concept and shares a geopolitical Caribbean solidarity with all the peoples of the archipelago regardless of their cultural differences. On the other hand, Creoleness is not a geographic concept but a "brutal interaction" of culturally different populations. New cultural designs are invented to allow for cohabitation, and as a result we see a non-harmonious mix of language, religion, and culinary. Creoleness is an original entity that emerges from this process after time and encompasses and perfects Americanness, because it is the mixing of these isolated cultures, thus making them no longer isolated (90-3).

16. This statement refers to Glissant's belief that "the idea of creolization demonstrates that henceforth it is no longer valid to glorify 'unique' origins that the race safeguards and prolongs. In Western tradition, genealogical descent guarantees racial exclusivity, just as Genesis legitimizes genealogy. To assert peoples are creolized, that creolization has value, is to deconstruct

in this way the category of 'creolized' that is considered as halfway between the two 'pure' extremes" (140).

Works Cited

Alexander, Jeffrey C. "Toward a Theory of Cultural Trauma." *Cultural Trauma and Collective Identity*. Eds. Jeffrey C. Alexander, Ron Eyerman, Bernhard Giesen, Neil J. Smelser, Piotr Sztompka. Berkeley: UP of California, 2004. 1-30. Print.

Anderson, Benedict. *Imagined Communities: Reflections on the Origin and Spread of Nationalism*. New York: Verso, 2006. Print.

Arce de Vázquez, Margot. "*Los soles truncos*: comedia trágica de René Marqués." *Sin Nombre* 10.3 (1979): 58-70. Print.

Arion, Frank Martinus. "The Great Curassow or the Road to Caribbeanness." *Caribbean Literature from Suriname, the Netherlands Antilles, Aruba, and the Netherlands*. Ed. Hilda van Neck-Yoder. Spec. Issue of *Callaloo* 21.3 (1998): 447-52. Print.

Arriví, Francisco. *Vejigantes*. San Juan: Editorial Cultural, 2001. Print.

Baldrich, Juan José. *Class and the State: The Origins of Populism in Puerto Rico, 1934-1952*. Diss. Yale U, 1981. Print.

Benítez Rojo, Antonio. *La isla que se repite: el Caribe y la perspectiva posmoderna*. Hanover: Ediciones del Norte, 1996. Print.

Bernabé, Jean, Patrick Chamoiseau, and Raphael Confiant. *In Praise of Creoleness*. Trans. M.B. Taleb-Khyar. Baltimore: John Hopkins UP, 1993. Print.

Briere, John N. *Child Abuse Trauma: Theory and Treatment of the Lasting Effects*. Newbury Park, CA: Sage Publications, 1992. Print.

Burrows, Victoria. *Whiteness and Trauma: The Mother-Daughter Knot in the Fiction of Jean Rhys, Jamaica Kincaid and Toni Morrison*. New York: Palgrave Macmillan, 2004. Print.

Cypress, Sandra M. "The Theater." A *History of Literature in the Caribbean*. Ed. A. James Arnold. Vol. 2. Amsterdam: John Benjamins Publishing Company. 239-262. Print.

Derrida, Jacques. *Margins of Philosophy*. Trans. Alan Bass. Chicago: UP of Chicago, 1982. Print.

Díaz Quiñones, Arcadio. *El almuerzo en la hierba*. Río Piedras: Ediciones Huracán, 1982. Print.

———. *Conversación con José Luis González*. Río Piedras: Ediciones Huracán, 1976. Print.

Felman, Shoshana. "Women and Madness: The Critical Phallacy." *What Does a Woman Want?: Reading and Sexual Difference.* Baltimore: The Johns Hopkins UP, 1993. 20-40. Print.

Gelpí, Juan. *Literatura y paternalismo en Puerto Rico.* Río Piedras: Editorial de la Universidad de Puerto Rico, 1993. Print.

Girard, René. "The Plague in Literature and Myth." *"To double business bound": Essays on Literature, Mimesis, and Anthropology.* Baltimore: The John Hopkins UP, 1978. 136-54. Print.

Glissant, Édouard. *Caribbean Discourse.* Trans. J. Michael Dash. Charlottesville: UP of Virginia, 1989. Print.

González, José Luis. *El país de cuatro pisos y otros ensayos.* San Juan: Ediciones Huracán, 1989. Print.

Handley, George B. "A New World Poetics of Oblivion." *Look Away! The U.S. South in New World Studies.* Eds. Deborah Cohn and Jon Smith. Durham: Duke UP, 2004. 25-51. Print.

———. *Postslavery Literatures in the Americas: Family Portraits in Black and White.* Ed. A. James Arnold. Charlottesville: UP of Virginia, 2000. Print.

Hirsh, Elizabeth and Gary A. Olson. "Je-Luce Irigaray": A Meeting with Luce Irigaray." *Women Writing Culture.* Eds. Gary Olson and Elizabeth Hirsh. Trans. Elizabeth Hirsh and Gaëtan Brulotte. 141-68. Print.

Holzapfel, Tamara. "The Theater of René Marqués." *Dramatists in Revolt: The New Latin American Theater.* Eds. Leon F. Lyday and George W. Woodyard. Austin: UP of Texas, 1976. 146-66. Print.

Irigaray, Luce. *Speculum of the Other Woman.* Trans. Gillian G. Gill. Ithaca, NY: Cornel UP, 1985. Print.

LaCapra, Dominick. *Writing History, Writing Trauma.* Baltimore: The Johns Hopkins UP, 2001. Print.

Lewis, Armanda. *The Ethical Orphan in the Nineteenth-Century Latin American Novel.* Diss. Columbia U, 2007. Ann Arbor: UMI, 2009. Print.

Loichot, Valérie. *Orphan Narratives: The Postplantation of Faulkner, Glissant, Morrison, and Saint-John Perse.* Ed. A. James Arnold. Charlottesville: UP of Virginia, 2007. Print.

Malena, Anne and Pascale de Souza. "Introduction." *Journal of Caribbean Literatures* 3.1 (2001): 4-10. Print.

Márques, René. "El puertorriqueño dócil (literatura y realidad psicológica)." *Ensayos (1953-1966).* San Juan: Editorial Antillana, 1966. 147-210. Print.

———. "Purificación en la calle del Cristo." San Juan: Editorial Cultural, 1983. 5-21. Print.

———. *Los soles truncos.* San Juan: Editorial Cultural, 1983. 23-84. Print.

Merton, Robert K. "Social Structure and Anomie." *Robert K. Merton on Social Structure and Science.* Ed. Piotr Sztompka. Chicago: UP of Chicago, 1996. 132–52. Print.

Náter, Miguel Ángel. *Los demonios de la duda: teatro existencialista hispano-americano.* San Juan: Isla Negra, 2004. Print.

O'Connell, Joanna. *Prospero's Daughter: The Prose of Rosario Castellanos.* Austin: UP of Texas, 1995. Print.

Pedreira, Antonio. *Insularismo.* Ed. Mercedes López-Baralt. San Juan: Editorial Plaza Mayor, 2001. Print.

Renan, Ernest. "What is a Nation? (1882)." *Nations and Identities: Classic Readings.* Ed. Vincent P. Pecora. Malden, MA: Blackwell, 2001. 162-76. Print.

Rhys, Jean. *Wide Sargasso Sea.* Ed. Judith L. Raiskin. New York: Norton & Company, 1999. Print.

Rodríguez Castro, María Elena and Silvia Alvarez-Curbelo. *Del nacionalismo al populismo: cultura y política en Puerto Rico.* Río Piedras: Ediciones Huracán, 1993. Print.

Russ, Elizabeth Christine. *The Plantation in the Postslavery Imagination.* New York: Oxford UP, 2009. Print.

Scarry, Elaine. *The Body in Pain: The Making and Unmaking of the World.* Oxford: Oxford UP, 1985. Print.

Smesler, Neil J. "Psychological Trauma and Cultural Trauma." *Cultural Trauma and Collective Identity.* Eds. Jeffrey C. Alexander, Ron Eyerman, Bernard Giesen, Neil J. Smelser, and Piotr Sztompka. Berkeley: UP of California, 2004. 31-59. Print.

Sontag, Susan. *Illness as Metaphor.* New York: Farrar, Straus and Giroux, 1977. Print.

Sztompka, Piotr. "The Trauma of Social Change: A Case of Postcommunist Societies." *Cultural Trauma and Collective Identity.* Eds. Jeffrey C. Alexander, Ron Eyerman, Bernhard Giesen, Neil J. Smelser, Piotr Sztompka. Berkeley: UP of California, 2004. 155-196. Print.

Vargas, Margarita. "Dreaming the Nation: René Marquéa's *Los soles truncos.*" *Latin American Theater Review* 37.2 (2004): 41-55. Print.

Vergès, Françoise. *Monsters and Revolutionaries: Colonial Family Romance and Métissage.* Durham: Duke UP, 1999. Print.

Whitehead, Anne. *Memory.* London: Routledge, 2009. Print.

Zenon Cruz, Isabelo. *Narciso descubre su trasero: el negro en la cultura puertorriqueña.* Humacao: Editorial Furidi, 1975. Print.

Creating Revolutionary Cuba's National Hero: The Cultural Capital of the *Cimarrón*

Lindsay Puente
University of Arkansas, Fayetteville

Traditional studies of modernity and revolution often neglect the importance of racial slavery in shaping the modern world. The dominant narrative of modernity elides the formative role of the slave system and colonialism altogether and especially silences the advances made possible by radical anti-slavery. Certainly there are revisionist narratives of modernity which emphasize the roles colonialism, the slave system, and acts of resistance have played in the development of modern nation-states. Likewise acts of radical anti-slavery have at times been included in official narratives of the state as positive foundational acts either for independence projects, abolition movements, or cross-Caribbean collaborative possibilities—but these treatments are often to translate these moments, actions, and actors into a modern, teleological schema that pre-supposes a universal notion of freedom and a universal goal of the formation of an independent nation-state. Radical anti-slavery, however, exists both within and beyond these modernity projects.

Hegemonic studies of modernity often prioritize the state as the only means through which political action is possible and thus deny slavery and radical acts of slave resistance their modernizing and political weight. For example, in their introduction to the collection *The Politics of Culture in the Shadow of Capital*, Lisa Lowe and David Lloyd indicate that when "political resistance could only be recognized as such insofar as it was organized through nationalisms that took as their object the capture of the colonial state and the formation of modern institutions and subjects," other forms of resistance—such as slave resistance—are patronized and denied political priority (4). However, even those acts which do not intend to overthrow the existing power, such as defection from the plantations to remote *cimarrón* communities, had destabilizing effects and shaped the development of modern state power in the colonial world.[1] Such acts of cultural perseverance are political and defy hegemonic attempts to eradicate difference and to deny both collective and individual subjectivity to those who fall outside of political representation. For instance, despite the general silencing of alternative communal narratives, there exists an abundance of slave narratives endorsed by the dominant culture in literature, history, sculpture, paintings, etc. Within these narratives of the struggles against slavery on the part of the slaves, singular, masculine figures are most often chosen to represent broad sectors, and their actions are subsumed into national narratives that naturalize the development of a modern state. These figures are chosen because they prioritize the political, they uphold patriarchal hierarchies, and they fit easily into national teleologies that provide a historical authenticity for newly-formed states. Hence, nations emerging from colonialism, or entering a new era of self-definition, have tried to correct the wide gaps in the popular archive by addressing the active role of slavery and of slave resistance in the creation of national culture and the continued impact of the cultures of slavery and of slave resistance on contemporary life. These corrections to the popular archive are accompanied by an intellectual appropriation of previously conquered, marginalized, and oppressed communities and their histories in support of the symbolic force which is the nation.

Through an examination of Cuban sociologist Miguel Barnet's *Biografía de un cimarrón*, a ethnographic oral history of the life of an ex-slave, I would like to consider the manners in which radical anti-slavery *have* been remembered with attention to *who* has taken the responsibility of textualizing these memories and *whom* these memories are purported to represent. Barnet's *Biografía* narrates the life of Esteban Montejo (circa 1860-1973), a man born into Cuban slavery at the end of the nineteenth century. The *Biografía* is a transcription of Montejo's spoken testimony of his experiences as a slave, as a fugitive, as a paid mill-worker, and as a revolutionary independence fighter which was published during his lifetime as a testament to the trajectory of Cuban national identity. To rescue his story and to make it known nationally and internationally represents the hegemonic cultural authority's desire to create a more representative national imaginary through the inclusion of radical black figures. This move circumvents both violent and political action on the part of traditionally unrepresented groups—here, of black populations—by creating a controlled space in which their history can be recognized as contributing to the formation of national culture and thus preventing another uprising like that of 1812.[2]

As transitioning nations attempt to culturally authorize their existence, a symbolic past is resurrected through cultural ritualization: the official recognition of 'traditional,' local values and practices, and the reproduction of these for easy consumption by citizens in the forms of national holidays, monuments, and even the naming of streets, plazas and schools. This ritualization constructs meaning, dramatizing historic knowledge to confirm foundational acts and origins and to provide images of stability, authority, and a natural progression to the current state. The nationalism that emerges proposes a historical continuity between the emergence of a people and its form of representation, i.e., the sovereignty of the state. This nation-state was the modern paradigm for political formations, and newly independent countries strove to adopt this model as the logical end to oppressive histories. It is in this vein that Barnet's *Biografía de un cimarrón* gives voice to alternative forms of resistance and to alternative narratives of nation by providing a public and national forum for the private, local stories of slavery to societies that have been desensitized to the very indebtedness of the construction of the modern nation to slavery despite their Westernized prioritization of the nation-state. *Biografía de un cimarrón* uses the reconstructed first-person testimony of Esteban Montejo to challenge the bourgeois cultural priorities that had made invisible the active roles of slavery and slave resistance in the emergence of a Cuban national identity.

THE CULTURAL CAPITAL OF THE *CIMARRÓN*

Esteban Montejo is a localized hero, representative of the Cuban national imaginary, in the form of a singular, masculine slave figure. The project, first of academics like Fernando Ortiz, and then of his student, Miguel Barnet, to include the contributions and experiences of radical slaves in the national archive recognizes the need for a redefinition and revaluation of the nation and for authentic representations of national content and history. Fidel Castro's Cuban revolution in 1959 promised to finally institutionalize the racial equality that Jose Martí had called for at the turn of the century. Miguel Barnet, thus, in the spirit of the Cuban revolution, and in line with Castro's 1961 speech "Palabras a los intelectuales," strikes out to do an ethnographic study of life in the slave barracks in colonial Cuba, and of the continued abundance of Afro-Cuban traditions in religious practices such as Santería.[3] Barnet's research brought him to Esteban Montejo, a man with 105 years of age whose memory encompassed a century of foundational moments in Cuban history, from a perspective which had never been considered in official history. Titled *Biografía de un cimarrón* and published in 1966, the work is structured as Esteban Montejo's first-person account, and along with Juan Manzano's *Autobiografía de un esclavo* is the best-known slave narrative of the Hispanic Caribbean and now an essential part of the canon of Cuban literature. This text purports to be living memory, a direct link from the colonial past to the national present, through the oral testimony of a *cimarrón*.

Why is it that the *cimarrón* is a favorite (Caribbean) post-colonial representation of the national endeavor and yet also an incomplete institutional memory? Slavery was for centuries a forsaken fact of colonial life: slaves were not citizens or subjects, and because of their non-political status, their impact on social and political events was discounted. The memory of slave resistance previously had depended on communal (unofficial) memory to pass from generation to generation. This lack of the recognition of the positive influence of slavery on the organization of daily social encounters has devalued the cultural and political contributions of the black community to national identity—this lack has insinuated that slavery and slaves did not help to shape the contemporary nation. But how to fill this lack, when within Euro-American thought, there are certain and careful criteria that must accompany the idealized public figure? In order to receive official recognition, and thus to be brought into the private homes of citizens via mass public distribution first within Cuba and then internationally, the actions of the extraordinary individual must meet the criteria of the national will. This is to say, a hero must ultimately strive for the betterment of the nation, either on the level of a particular national plight, or on a larger level, such as that of liberty. Not only must a hero's political goals conform to those of the state, but also his/her personal and moral endeavors must be acceptable: generally, this hero should be Christian, literate and modern. While Esteban Montejo was illiterate, the textualization of his narrative made his story available to the reading public. His participation in the war for independence, his identification as a Cuban national, and his engagement with Christianity—albeit alongside an acknowledgement of African deities—make him an appropriate candidate for canonization in the Cuban national imaginary.

In the opening paragraphs to the narrative, we are introduced to an eclectic character who seems to truly mix Western and non-Western values. A reader of the original Spanish text would immediately note the distinct syntax and vocabulary that stylizes the narrative and reflects the education and culture of Afro-Cubans at the turn of the century, including the use of antiquated word forms and simplistic sentence structures. This non-normative syntax is combined with the detail of the speaking voice to form what I call *estebanismos*, which are overlaid and privileged throughout the narration. The very first line is captivating: "Hay cosas que yo no me explico de la vida" (15). After this profound statement, our narrator, Esteban Montejo, begins to list natural phenomena that he has witnessed in his life and the effects of these strange occurrences on men and animals alike. This leads us to his understanding of the supernatural: Christ is a god that is not African, but from nature, just as are other strange and powerful phenomena, and also African gods. His casual ability to bring these forms of belief together is the marker of his truthfulness, of his authenticity, and of his status as an Afro-Cuban creole. His mixture of Western and folk knowledge points to the authenticity of his first statement, that there are things that he cannot explain in life. And yet, he does not doubt the strangeness of a life that is the product of multiple world views crashing together in an island in the Caribbean under the colonial system. As such the constructed testimonial voice of the subject is an authentic and relatable Afro-Cuban representative who does not directly challenge the white Cuban elite position.

Not only does the narrator's casual attitude to the phenomena of life build his believability as a common and original individual, but the stream-of-consciousness organization that builds his monologue adds to this effect. The narrating voice, attributed entirely in the original version to Esteban Montejo, moves seamlessly from the inexplicable to nature, from natural gods to African gods, from Africa and the beginning of the slave trade to the abolition of slavery in Cuba.[4] And then, immediately following this stream of causal events and thoughts, we are given the ultimate truth-claim of the text: "A mí nada de eso se me borra. Lo tengo todo vivido. Hasta me acuerdo que mis padrinos me dijeron la fecha en que yo nací. Fue el 26 de diciembre de 1860, el día de San Esteban. Por eso me llamo Esteban" (16). Again, it is his very mixing of Western and folk knowledge that creates a voice that is intimate and realistic. The use of oral history ("mis padrinos me dijeron") and of a Western calendar ("el 26 de diciembre de 1860, el día de San Esteban") make this voice both one that the reader can relate to and one mired in verifiable data. It is the confident inconsistency of this voice—the matter-of-fact attitude that recognizes without question the phenomena of nature, that wonders at the phenomena of slavery, and that rationalizes the phenomenon of his very naming—that solidifies the image of non-Western difference being made knowable through textualization for the Western literate audience.

As Esteban recounts his personal memories of his childhood, we see a dependence on communal knowledge to develop individual identity: his understanding of his parentage comes from the words given to him from his godparents; his familiarity with his godparents comes from an acquaintance who introduced him to them after abolition and before the war. Despite this late introduction to his godparents (he would have been in his 30s when he met them), his respect for their memories is unshakable. He adopts their words as truth and remembers his parents through their words: "Claro que yo no vide [sic] a ese hombre nunca, pero sé que es positivo ese cuento porque me lo hicieron mis padrinos. Y a mí nada de lo que ellos me contaban se me ha olvidado" (17). We see immediately the excruciating familial separations that slavery forced upon its victims and the ensuing crises of identity that result from such violent amputations. The narrator has gained the reader's attention with his eclectic voice, the reader's trust with his confident originality, and the reader's sympathy as well, as the dehumanizing process of slavery is broken down to a personal but not entirely sour fact of life. Yet all of these trials have not broken Esteban Montejo. He is not disheartened, he is not embittered, and thus he does not frighten the white elite reader whose ancestors may well have participated in his oppression.

The narrator's voice establishes authenticity, a verifiable and material truth, early on through the use of specific names of places and people, precise dates, and of equipment and punishments identified with the sugar plantations of the late nineteenth century. His description of life in slavery is divided (in the original Spanish version) into three parts: a general introduction to slavery, a description of life in the slave barracks, and life in the wilderness as a runaway. The careful and specific details that accompany his musings work as supporting evidence to his personal experience with the mechanisms of slavery, from the nurseries to the work schedule to the living conditions, which serve to paint a more intimate picture of the inequality of these systems (the very systems that the new regime, that of Fidel Castro, had set out to destroy) than his reading audience would have ever encountered. Thus Esteban Montejo's personal memories and detailed familiarity, alongside the careful and deliberate editing and ordering of the narrative on the part of the Miguel Barnet, work to build the reader's trust in Montejo's experiences of the horrors of slavery and to elicit the reader's sympathy when, just a few pages into the narrative, Montejo gives voice to the memory of his first attempt to escape. The title of the text, the visual and sentient details of life on the plantation, the distinctive voice of the narrator, and the careful editing that constructs the text all works to establish reader interest and sympathy through the textual authenticity. These meticulous efforts crescendo until they bring the audience the first concrete instance of *cimarronaje* (I say concrete to differentiate from earlier in the text when Esteban discusses some of the consequences of his *cimarrón* status: he never knew his parents, etc) with the hope of having hooked the readers: "De lo que sí estoy seguro es que de allí me huí una vez; me reviré, carajo, y me huí. ¡Quién iba a querer trabajar!" (18). This imaginary bond between the audience—citizens who have never experienced slavery but eagerly consume the proof of its evil—and the narrating voice—which inhabits the spirit of rebellion—only grows stronger through the retelling of a desperate attempt to escape the physical and psychological shackles of slavery. This first attempt to escape oppression is quickly thwarted, and in a manner so harsh that even over 80 years later, the narrator-victim, Esteban Montejo, has sentient memories of the punishment: "Pero me cogieron mansito, y me dieron una de grillos que si me pongo a pensar bien los vuelvo a sentir. Me los amarraron fuertes y me pusieron a trabajar, con ellos y todo. Uno dice eso ahora y la gente no lo cree. Pero yo lo sentí y lo tengo que decir" (18). Alongside this first fulfillment of the promise of the title, an instance of *cimarronaje* which has previously been elided from national history, the frustrations of the violent power imbalance that is slavery are illustrated as the escape is thwarted. Here also, the reader is directly addressed by the narrating voice, as Montejo/Barnet appeal to the sympathies of the audience directly with claims to authenticity and this urgent need to testify to the atrocities of slavery. In this address, the narrator admits the incredulity of his story, especially to a contemporary audience, but reaffirms its truth and the need to tell—to witness—that very incredulity to that same naïve audience. In this way, *Biografía de un cimarrón* becomes the cultural capital needed to fill the holes in the academic and national archive surrounding slavery and active resistance to slavery.

Singular Examples: The Elision of Community

Miguel Barnet went to great lengths to present a social scientific text to the reading audience of Castro's newly won Cuba. Following the current standards, his text is accompanied with an introductory prologue that outlines the methodology of data accumulation; it is ordered in a clear and rational chronological fashion; it is accompanied by a series of notes from secondary sources that serve to corroborate the primary narrative; and finally, it is followed by a list of terms that serves to indicate that the original text is indeed the original, and that the idioms of Esteban Montejo were left intact, with a glossary of Afro-Cuban words and phrases to help the individual reader decipher the narrative/testimony of this unique survivor of Cuban history. In his reflective essay "La novela testimonio: socio-literatura" published in 1969, Barnet defines the ethnographic historical narrative as one that must reflect reality, and reflect the social relations of a nation, thus rescuing the past to explain (itself) to the present (109). The story of Esteban Montejo is particularly apt for Barnet, but there is a contradiction inherent in Barnet's fascination with both the possibility of the emergence of collective memory, and with Esteban Montejo as exemplary of this memory, as the seed from which this memory can grow: "Esteban, el Cimarrón, era un informante más, entre otros ancianos. Pero su vida era singular, completaba capítulos desconocidos, inéditos de la historia de Cuba y sus vivencias eran . . . únicas" ("Novela testimonio" 107). Herein lies the subterfuge, conscious or not, of employing the story of Esteban Montejo and of labeling him in particular as a *cimarrón* to fill in this lacuna of Cuban history: the memories of Esteban are specifically *not collective*, and it is this uniqueness that draws Barnet to him. While he has, as Barnet points out, participated in some of the most determinative events in Cuban history and does have memory of experiences not included in the Cuban canon, at the same time, his life has been exceptional and is marked specifically by a solitary and uncommon lifestyle. This is a repetition of the claim that Barnet makes in the introduction to the text: "La necesidad de verificar datos, fechas, u otros pormenores, nos llevó a sostener conversaciones con veteranos más o menos coetáneos con [Montejo]. Sin embargo, ninguno de ellos era de tan avanzada edad como para haber vivido etapas o hechos de los relatados por Esteban" (*Biografía* 8). The collective voice of Montejo's contemporaries is thrown aside in favor of a singular and exceptional voice, one that does not truly promote community or rebellion on a revolutionary level as a slave and a runaway, despite the rebellious connotations that accompany the use of the word *cimarrón* in the title of the biography.

The exceptionality of Esteban Montejo's narrative is evident within the text itself, as Barnet's own notes to the text reference the tendency of runaway slaves to form alternative communities, or *palenques*, once they entered the *monte*. Barnet quotes two sources to substantiate Montejo's narration of his experiences living in a cave (46, 225 n9): the first is taken from Antonio Núñez Jiménez's text *La gesta libertadora* (1961), which claims that caves were often used by runaways for the protection that these offered.[5] This same quotation also offers us the following information: "Los cimarrones fugitivos que obedecían a impulsos individuales de libertad pronto se convirtieron en grupos organizados para resistir a los amos, así nacieron los palenques, formados por grupos de negros que unas veces vivían en lomerías abruptas o en las cavernas apartadas" (225 n9). The second quotation is taken from the *Memorias de la Real Sociedad Patriótica de La Habana* (1839) and describes the manner in which caves were often used by fugitive slaves for shelter. It details a particular cave, similar to that which Esteban describes, which had failed the fugitives because it had only one entrance, allowing the fugitives to be smoked out by their pursuers. These notes serve to substantiate Montejo's claim to have lived in a cave, but they also highlight the tendency of *cimarrones* to form communities in the *monte*. Our narrator, however, lives in absolute solitude during his time as a fugitive in the wilderness. In fact, he refutes the idea of joining a *cimarrón* community, stressing his individuality and claiming that he felt safer on his own: "Muchas cosas no las hacía. Por mucho tiempo no hablé ni una palabra con nadie. . . . Otros cimarrones andaban siempre de dos o tres. Pero eso era un peligro, porque cuando llovía, el rastro de los pies se quedaba en el fango. Así cogieron a muchos grupitos bobos" (49). Thus even within Barnet's text we are presented with the non-representativeness of Montejo's narrative. Esteban Montejo's experience of slavery and of *cimarronaje* was exceptional for the solitude that defined it.

When our narrator tells of life in the *barracones*, we see a glimpse of the tight-knit community that dominated the slaves' social system. There is a strict division of labor within the domestic sphere (22), there is a communal effort to raise children (17-18, 22, 23), and there is creative use of leisure time (25-27). One of the communal pastimes that Montejo recounts for us was a religious game called *mayombe*, which is perhaps one of the greatest examples we are given of the type of alternative social organization that the imported Africans and their descendants maintained. The game involved invoking the spirits with the use of drums, songs, and small offerings. Once the spirits were engaged in the ceremony, the participants could ask for various blessings. In the spirit of communal rebellion, this same game was often used against the colonial system: "Cuando el amo castigaba a algún esclavo, los demás recogían un poquito de tierra y la metían en la cazuela. Con esa tierra resolvían lo que querían. Y el amo se enfermaba o pasaba algún daño en la familia. Porque mientras la tierra esa estaba dentro de la cazuela el amo estaba apresado ahí y ni el diablo lo sacaba. Esa era la venganza del congo con el amo" (27). This small moment in the text demonstrates that the community of slaves defended each of its members, even from within the system, using unique and creative mixtures of non-Western belief systems, and that from the point of view of these actors, this resistance was active and effective. However, even in these moments, the narrator maintains a careful distance from the events he describes, taking an informed outsider perspective, rather than one of an initiated participant.

It is not until Esteban Montejo begins to relate his experiences with the *chicherekú* that he becomes personally involved in the story that he narrates. Unlike his recounting of the celebrations, the religious practices, and the music, of which he gives an impersonal impression with a few time-markers for authenticity and verifiability, when he begins to remember the *chicherekú* he brings first person encounters and relived fear into his narrative:

> Pero de Flor de Sagua me acuerdo del chicherekú. El chicherekú era conguito de nación. No hablaba español. Era

un hombrecito cabezón que salía corriendo por los barracones, brincaba y le caía a uno detrás. Yo lo vide muchas
veces. Y lo oí chillar que parecía una jutía. Eso es positivo
y hasta en el Porfuerza, hasta hace pocos años, existía uno
que corría igual. La gente le salía huyendo porque decían
que era el mismo diablo y que estaba ligado con *mayombe*
y con muerto. Con el chicherekú no se puede jugar porque
hay peligro. A mí en verdad no me gusta mucho hablar de
él, porque yo no lo he vuelto a ver más, y sí por alguna
casualidad . . . bueno, ¡el diablo son las cosas! (34)

This personal memory of the *chicherekú* is an example of those
moments, few and far between though they may be, that capture
the attention of the audience and, through his careful, rational and
detailed descriptions, build the credibility of Esteban Montejo, *cimarrón*. He is not so intimate with the stories that he recounts as to seem
particularly prejudiced about them, but rather recounts these incidents
from a distance creating a scientific feeling around the histories. And
yet, the audience needs moments of intimacy from the narrator to
highlight the privileged insider view provided in this unique narration.
It is these moments of 'irrationality' that maintain the harmlessness
of the former slave: he does not threaten the sensibilities of his white
readers with finger-pointing, nor does he attempt to recruit them to
his non-Western ways. For the part of the narrator, we feel a sort
of desperation to recapture the moment of his encounters with the
chicherekú, and the eeriness that this figure invokes. Our narrator
gives multiple personal truth-markers in this passage ("yo lo vide," "lo
oí," "es positivo," "en verdad"), and even pulls from contemporary
folklore ("hasta hace pocos años") in an attempt to give an accurate
description of the emotional memories evoked at recalling this African
figure, this "conguito de nación." While these moments give the reader
a glimpse of an alternative world-view, they are so infrequent that they
are not the focus of the text, but rather serve to essentialize and lend a
commercial authenticity to the character that emerges in the narration,
easily consumed by the reading public.

Barnet positions Esteban Montejo as an individual that will
inspire and lead the masses, a la Che Guevara's 'hombre nuevo,' and
thus the easy consumption of the narration is an important factor in
the success of the text. However, there are moments when Esteban

Montejo's exceptionality could make him suspect as a national hero, or as a representation of the essence of Cubanidad: the most notable of these is Montejo's refusal/inability to enter into a hetero-normative relationship. But he is able to significantly establish his masculinity and his heterosexuality in spite of his prolonged celibacy, so that the narrative maintains a strong masculine figure with a unique and individual voice for these bizarre and unimaginable adventures. Montejo's simple yet profound musings about these adventures maintain an air of authenticity, rendering the folk subject intelligible for the elite audience.

In the wilderness, Montejo seems only to have truly lacked access to hetero-normative sex:

> La pura verdad es que a mí nunca me faltó nada en el monte. La única cosa que no podía hacer era el sexo. Como no había mujeres, tenía que quedarme con el gusto recogido. Ni con las yeguas se podía pisar porque relinchaban que parecían demonios. Y cuando los guajiros oían ese alboroto venían en seguida y a mí nadie me iba a poner los grillos por una yegua. (53-54)

Thus Montejo is forced to sacrifice all forms of sexual intercourse for his freedom quest. His impulses to hetero-normative masculinity urge him to opt for celibacy rather than homosexual sex or bestiality, and thus ensure that his audience is able to continue to fully esteem him. In this way, his celibacy actually increases his masculine identity and creates a figure that is almost unimaginably dedicated to the cause of personal freedom.

This masculinity that is established early in the text, despite his celibacy, is essential to the image of the *cimarrón* and to Esteban Montejo's identity not just as a *cimarrón* but also as a soldier in the Cuban war for independence, and thus as the quintessential Afro-Cuban subject. Montejo's narrative is presented as the missing link in Cuban history, the definitive piece that completes the story from multiple perspectives in the new era of post-revolution Cuba. In this narrative, the oppression of the colonial Spanish and the oppression of the class system that demands the forced labor of a people are best defined through the figure of a rebellious and virile man who would forsake even sexual relations in order to preserve his freedom.

However, the elision of the feminine perspective and voice is one that is consciously brought about by choices made by the editor, Miguel Barnet, as his introduction to the text clearly indicates. While perhaps Montejo's own experiences were limited, Barnet was presented with the ability to include other voices, including feminine voices, in his study (5). The combination of Montejo's objectification of women throughout the text (35, 37, 41), and Barnet's elision of women from his study result in a systematic denial of woman-as-subject for the sake of an intelligible, masculine, independent and authentic voice that speaks for the Afro-Cuban experience in the process of Cuban history.

Singular Examples: Consumable Difference

The literary and cultural move to make a more inclusive national archive through the inclusion of the contributions and experiences of radical slaves recognizes the need for a redefinition and revaluation of the nation and of 'authentic' representations. In the case of Cuba, this meant writing counter-narratives to older bourgeois history in order to bring the past into the present and promote the 'nuevo hombre revolucionario' as a particularly Cuban development of Marxist ideology (Moreno Fraginals 55-56, Arroyo 204). The ethnographic work of Miguel Barnet opened the ground for a new genre, the *testimonio*, which exposed this crisis and limitation of bourgeois knowledge. *Testimonio*, a devaluation of literature and high culture as elitist and exclusionary cultural practices, is a push toward multiculturalism, a push for more inclusive and complete representation. However, it brings along with it a paradox: Western disciplinary knowledge cannot expose its own failures to be universal from within that very same system of knowledge. Within attempts to bring non-traditional, and even oppositional, subjects into *traditional* academic discourse, if the subject is approached as other, the discourse maintains a necessary distance from that other, thus reproducing Western academic systems of knowledge. When the subject is translated into the vocabulary of that exclusive system of knowledge, on the other hand, original difference is subsumed for the sake of a hegemonic sameness.

I am asking, through this reading of Miguel Barnet's *Biografía de un cimarrón*, that we interrogate the production of historical narrative in authoritative forms. *Testimonio* as a genre has been the subject of numerous debates within the academy, built around questions of truth and representation. Latin Americanist critic John Beverley, in his book *Subalternity and Representation: Arguments in Cultural Theory*, has approached this debate by questioning the power of the academy. This approach allows us to consider the nature of these debates over *testimonio*: perhaps they are actually an attempt by a traditional academy to hold on to traditional (Western reason/scientific rationality) understandings of truth and reality. While debates have raged around the verifiable truth of the events narrated in testimonies such as *Me llamo Rigoberta Menchú y así me nació la conciencia* and *Biografía de un cimarrón*, the problem is not the *truth* of these testimonials, but the need on the part of social scientists to present these truths, to represent this knowledge, in the language of the Western academy and under the guise of the Western intellectual understanding of truth. In this case, the problem is not ever Montejo's story, and the accuracy or gaps that are included there, nor the manner in which these stories emerged (with an audience, with small bribes of tobacco and women, with food, etc) but rather is the manner in which they are dispersed and then left open to criticism from an institution that has a fundamentally different understanding of truth and memory.[6] The question then becomes whether our social scientist, our translator and transcriber, ever truly was able to understand the fundamental *difference* that s/he became privy to in the opportunity to hear these stories. I argue that, in fact, this process of transcription is a subsuming of difference into an exoticized version of the same.

It is this subsuming of difference that has allowed for the canonization of *Biografía* as a celebration of difference and a testament to new levels of cultural inclusion in Cuba and the Americas. In the original and in translation, *Biografía de un cimarrón* is a highly anthologized slave narrative, which now makes up a part of both the Cuban and the Caribbean canon. Montejo's narrative is an exemplar of runaway slave narratives in the Caribbean, just as the rebellious slave is exemplar of the spirit of the Caribbean itself. Much of the excitement that surrounds this text derives from the novelty of the survivor story, and of finding a survivor of slavery half a century after its end. As a particularly Cuban text, *Biografía* becomes representative of the attempts that accompanied the Cuban Revolution to syncretize race on the island and to write Afro-Cuban identity into the national narrative. Thus, selections of the text appear in Cuban literary anthologies in English and Spanish, discussions of *testimonio*, critical approaches to slave narratives, and general introductions to Caribbean literature. While in part this speaks to the paucity of primary source information from which to create scholarly studies, it also speaks to the willingness of the academy to gloss over this loss of information, and to readily and uncritically accept this specialized figure as representative of a larger phenomenon.

Thus, post-revolution Cuba coincides with a deprecation of the value of the literary as ambiguous, elusive, false and aesthetic, to produce a turn to the "documentary novel" so that *testimonio* emerges, narrating what Roberto González Echevarria labels "presentness" in the insightful article *"Biografía de un cimarrón* and the Novel of the Cuban Revolution." This "presentness" is an attempt to overcome the temporal and material mediation that is writing. Testimonial writing brings the past into the present, and creates an image of the present as a part of an on-going historical process. This is done by bringing the memory of the past into present discourse, and thus bringing individual experience into collective memory.[7] Memory, as with its narrativization, is always mediated by time, by the very act of its inscription/telling. And yet it is this mediation that *testimonio* seeks to dispel, thus purporting to provide a more truthful, more immediate account than would otherwise be available.

The collective memory that the *testimonio* seeks to create emerges through the truth-claims of the text—the minor details, the *estebanismos*, and the privileged point of view reinforce the narrator's immediacy and erase the acts of writing and of mediating. This privileged voice then becomes oral tradition, becomes collective memory, through the voice of the everyday, drawing coherent and tangible lines from now to then, from present to past. This gesture towards the 'we,' towards the collective, towards the past within the present, the tangible, meaningful past, is what Miguel Barnet finds in Esteban Montejo and his story.

These *estebanismos* occur at regular intervals throughout the text. They do not override the narrative at any point, as too much would be unintelligible, but are just present enough to provide an aura of authenticity. These are a combination of seemingly banal but inventive observations, which seem incidental, because they do not work to advance the narrative, but provide insight into the unique consciousness of our narrator: "Había más tabernas que niguas en el monte" (27); "Pelaba como lo hacen hoy. Y nunca dolía, porque el pelo es lo más raro que hay; aunque uno ve que crece y todo, está muerto" (32); "Mientras más me acercaba a la costa más grande se iba poniendo. Yo siempre me figuré que el mar era un río gigante" (56). These observations, juxtaposed with strategic markers of time, ("A mí, por ejemplo, no se me olvida más" (31); "que yo no he vuelto a ver" (32); "Yo digo esto porque da por resultado que yo lo vide mucho en la esclavitud" (35), and arbitrary details, such as phonetic descriptions of birdcalls, personalize the narrative (56-58). It is unlikely that the transcription of these birdcalls, for example, will give us an accurate phonetic account of the sounds that Esteban uttered, let alone heard, half a century before this moment of utterance, but their inclusion in the text is a very specific tool that builds the character and voice of our narrator by giving us an impression of his attention to detail and his memory of the most minor events in his long life. Montejo's desire to repeat for us even the sounds that he heard during his life as a runaway demonstrates a commitment to his audience and to his narrative, and the commitment of the intellectuals of the Cuban Revolution to bring these previously marginalized and ignored experiences to the forefront of Cuban culture.

Yet, as we have seen, Montejo is not an accurate subject for collective memory, although he does move beyond Westernized modern conceptions. Rather, he is representative of the unique. The question that remains to be asked, then, is why is this memory the one that is canonized? By favoring the singular history of Esteban Montejo, Barnet dismisses the history of the formation of complex *cimarrón* communities in Cuba and in Latin America. His subject negates the multiple experiences of Africans and their descendants in the Americas in the colonial slave system and the forms of resistance and survival that were unique to this consciousness. Instead, Barnet's work reduces resistance to a form that translates easily into the current national agenda and that is exemplified by a single and exceptional man. The active denial of the resistance to forced labor is covered over with the canonization of the story of this exceptional *cimarrón*. In this way, the history of slavery and resistance is written into the Cuban narrative. In this Cuban narrative, however, true and violent revolution is only permissible against an outside force—in this case Spanish rule—and not against the Cuban *criollos* that employ enslaved labor to run their mills.

The inclusion and longevity of *Biografía de un cimarrón* within the cultural archive is not just a move to naturalize the revolutionary nature of the image of Cuba, nor simply to incorporate individual and personal voices in the Cuban archive. It is also a move to racially desegregate Cuba by bringing to life the reality of slavery within the Cuban narrative. Thus it is significant that the title of the book is *Biografía de un cimarrón*, or biography of a runaway slave, rather than of a revolutionary, despite the fact that the majority of Montejo's life is lived in post-slavery, and that only a quarter of the narrative is dedicated to Montejo's life within slavery and as a runaway in the bush. The cultural capital of the denomination of *cimarrón* thus must be considered in this formative history-in-the-present, as it allows for the translation and homogenization of a large sector of society into the representation of a single figure that is packaged for public consumption, and devalues the experience of Africans and their descendants in the Americas and the forms of resistance and survival that were unique to this consciousness.

CONCLUSION

The revalued figure of the rebellious slave is meant to represent a history of resistance to Western (white) oppression that was previously elided. However, such figures are chosen for their translatability and familiarity to the very audiences that they seem to resist. Despite representing active resistance to forces of oppression, these revalued figures fit neatly into westernized molds of the national hero. Montejo becomes the ideal figure of resistance because his resistance is not destructive to the progress of the nation. Montejo, however, was not a typical representation of *cimarronaje*. He was by all accounts moderate in terms of his rebellion against slavery and the colonial system. In fact, the *Biografía* only dedicates a small portion of the narrative to Montejo's life as a slave and a fugitive. The version of the past that resurfaces is that which supports contemporary national ideology. Yet, if we are to pay homage to the achievements of a fundamentally non-Western derived people in the destruction of the Westernized versions of the institutions of slavery and colonialism as they were transferred to the Caribbean islands, can a figure that so neatly fits into a Western mode of thought be truly representative? Does such a desire to fit a Western intellectual mold accurately reflect the history of struggles against Western colonialism and slavery by the oppressed in the Caribbean?

My point here is that those figures that are less intelligible to Western-trained intellectual thought—such as the collectives that formed runaway slave communities—are hidden from national discourse. This is often due to the paucity of adequate primary sources, a dearth which makes a discussion of the intent of these historical actors a drifting and nebulous goal. Instead, individual figures such as Esteban Montejo are elected to represent struggles against both oppression and national history. These figures produce idealist explanations of these liberation struggles, explanations which often conform to politicized nation-building myths that do not account for the difference that these actors embody. The masses and those who sought alternatives to Europeanized forms of state and community are either overlooked or are subsumed into a cause that has been translated into our contemporary idea of nation. This subsumption prevents continued challenges to the now accepted forms of governance and distributions of power and perpetuates the uncritical veneration of Western political forms, therefore continuing to cast a shadow of shame on those individuals who suffered the indignities of slavery.

Only those acts which were perpetuated with the specific goal of independence or which resulted in independence are given sociohistorical weight. Those acts of resistance which did not have as their goal replacement governments for the colonial system, but instead sought alternative communal forms, such as maroon communities, are disappeared. The singular, masculine, and easily narrativizable figures—which are those most often chosen to embody the struggles against slavery on the part of the slaves—represent diverse communities, and their actions are subsumed into modern national narratives. These figures are chosen because they prioritize the political, they uphold patriarchal hierarchies, and they fit easily into national teleologies that provide a historical authenticity to newly-formed states.

This essay is a consideration of the production of historical narrative in authoritative forms. History is the textualization of the past, and this textualization usually takes a chronological, political-material narrative form. Memory, on the other hand, is imperfect, fragmented, and non-linear. What is lost when we try to historicize memory? When we work beyond the archive, we enter into the realm of memory—a realm that has been traditionally marginalized from official history for its imperfections and fragmentations. Not only is popular memory imperfect, it lacks relevance to the ruling classes which have archival evidence of the historical narratives they wish to perpetuate. When we try to represent that which the archive has denied, and in doing so we critique the knowledge produced behind that denial, what does that leave us with? A paradox. As we try to expose the failure of a system of knowledge that claims to be universal from within that very system of knowledge, a different problem arises. Traditional discourse has left out the narratives of difference—of the subaltern, of the other—because these narratives are unintelligible. When we continue to approach this subject without acknowledging its difference, but instead translate it into a form compatible to our system of knowledge (linear, singular narrative history), we come no closer to representing what has been left out. An adhesion to a scientific historical form cannot represent a subject that refuses that same form. On the other hand, only attempts to narrativize the experience of the radical slave from within, not by translating the unfamiliar into familiar terms such as revolution and nation and Jacobin, but by considering alternative systems of value, communication and community, alternative notions of gender, leadership and freedom, will offer a possible representation that does not assume easy consumption, but that admits uncertainty and difference and that does not instrumentalize this representation for contemporary socio-political goals and does not orientalize the subject.

Notes

1. *Cimarrón* is a term coined by the colonial Spanish to denominate a runaway slave. Its literal meaning refers to cattle that have strayed and now live wild off the land. Within the system of slavery, a *cimarrón* is a runaway slave; *cimarronaje* is the act of flight. The British adopted and anglicized the term: maroon. I use the original term *cimarrón* throughout this work to denote the international nature of the system of slavery and the international collaborations against slave rebellion in the Caribbean.

2. Following the successes of the Haitian Revolution at the turn of the century (1792-1804), colonial governments of slave societies such as Cuba lived in constant fear of another Haiti. In attempts to prevent violence and rebellion, news of the success of the revolution and veneration of the black Haitian leaders were strictly suppressed. This suppression backfired, however, as José Antonio Aponte, a free black artisan from Havana, then circulated images of these rebellious leaders to inspire fear in the colonial government and to inspire pride and consciousness on the part of the oppressed.

Ultimately, the suppression of the success of the slaves in Haiti led directly to a violent conspiracy against the government and a slave uprising. The continued demonization of rebellious slaves and their ancestors who fought against the injustices of slavery fomented continued conspiracies and uprisings throughout the 19th century. See: Matt D. Childs' article in *The Impact of the Haitian Revolution in the Atlantic World*, edited by David P. Geggus, 2001 or Elzbieta Sklodowska's *Espectros y espejismos: haití en el imaginario cubano.*

3. In his June 1961 speech to the intellectuals, Castro claimed "dentro de la Revolución, todo; contra la Revolución, nada" in a call for artistic and intellectual production that would clearly reflect the goals of the revolution, and thus represent the people of Cuba.

4. It is worth noting, of course, that the organization of the text actually results from the inventions and manipulations of Miguel Barnet, whose heavy-handed editing is now openly acknowledged within academic discourse. But at the time of its release, the role of the transcriber was assumed to be transparent, and this is still the standing assumption in many of the anthologized editions of the text, which neglect to include a note on the conditions of production of the text.

5. Antonio Núñez Jiménez (1923-1998) was an influential anthropologist who was also well known for his participation alongside Che Guevara in the Cuban Revolution, and who occupied many influential government positions in the post-revolutionary period.

6. For an elaboration on this point, see Amy Nauss Millay's *Voices from the fuente viva: The Effect of Orality in Twentieth-Century Spanish American Narrative.*

7. Gonzalez Echevarría explains that to bring writing into the present—to capture the chaos of the moment, and the fragmentation of the actual experience—is to ensure that memory is preserved. At this moment, "[w]riting hovers on that point where memory slips away from the present to become literature, a code that is both memory and the gesture of its recovery. Once it becomes literature, memory may return to the present, but (already) only and always belatedly, having relinquished its immediacy in the process" (253).

Works Cited

Arroyo, Jossianna. *Travestismos culturales: literatura y etnografía en Cuba y Brasil*. Pittsburgh: IILI-Serie Nuevo Siglo, 2003. Print.

Barnet, Miguel. *Biografía de un cimarrón*. La Habana: Ediciones Unión, 1967. Print.

———. "La novela testimonio: socio-literatura" *Unión* [Havana] 6.4 (1969): 99-122. Print.

———. "Testimonio y comunicación: una vía hacia la identidad." *Unión* [Havana] 19.4 (1980): 99-122. Print.

Beverly, John. *Subalternity and Representation: Arguments in Cultural Theory.* Durham: Duke University Press, 1999. Print.

Castro, Fidel. "Palabras a los intelectuales: Discurso pronunciado por el Comandante Fidel Castro Ruz, primer ministro del gobierno revolucionario y secretario del PURSC, como conclusion de las reuniones con los intelectuales cubanos, efectuadas en la Biblioteca Nacional el 16, 23 y 30 de junio de 1961." Ministerio de Cultura de la República. *Ministerio de Cultura de la República.* Web. 14 April 2012.

Gonzalez Echevarria, Roberto. "'Biografia de un cimarrón' and the Novel of the Cuban Revolution." *NOVEL: A Forum on Fiction.* 13.3 (1980): 249-263. Print.

Geggus, David P. *The Impact of the Haitian Revolution in the Atlantic World.* Colombia, SC: U of South Carolina Press, 2001. Print.

Guevara, Ernesto. *El socialismo y el hombre nuevo.* México: Siglo Veintiuno, 1977. Print.

Lowe, Lisa and David Lloyd. Introduction. *The Politics of Culture in the Shadow of Capital.* Eds. Lisa Lowe and David Lloyd. Durham: Duke UP, 1997. 1-32. Print.

Moreno Fraginals, Manuel. "La historia como arma." *Órbita de Manuel Moreno Fraginals.* Ed. Alfredo Prieto. La Habana: Ediciones Unión, 2009. 53-67. Print.

Nauss Millay, Amy. *Voices from the* fuente viva: *The Effect of Orality in Twentieth-Century Spanish American Narrative.* Lewisburg, Penn: Bucknell University Press, 2005. Print.

Sklodowska, Elzbieta. *Espectros y espejismos: Haití en el imaginario cubano.* Madrid: Iberoamericana, 2009. Print.

La Habana de Pedro Juan Gutiérrez y Antonio José Ponte: el mapa de una ciudad marginal

Damaris Puñales-Alpízar
Case Western Reserve University

A partir de la narración de espacios subalternos, constituidos por prácticas humanas marginales que están, o han estado, fuera de la historia oficial de la nación, gran parte de la narrativa cubana de las últimas décadas da cuenta de una geografía de la subalternidad que contradice los logros sociales en los cuales se ha sustentado, al menos a nivel del discurso, la Revolución cubana. Personajes al margen de la ley y de la sociedad en todo sentido, edificios que se derrumban, relaciones interpersonales como transacciones monetarias, una ciudad como prisión y otros temas del fracaso del proyecto social revolucionario pueblan muchas de las novelas cubanas que se publican hoy día dentro y fuera de la isla.

Al margen de lo rentable, más a nivel afectivo que efectivo, que puedan resultar tales narrativas de lo subalterno, esta literatura informa de un espacio material decadente y ruinoso que es a su vez mímesis de un proyecto social disfuncional. Estas narrativas trazan el mapa de una ciudad, de un país, cuya escritura física del espacio geográfico, arquitectónico y humano no encaja en la visión hegemónica y monocromática que tradicionalmente se ha ofrecido desde el poder. Los personajes que pueblan estas historias son la antítesis del "hombre nuevo" que debía haber formado el proceso revolucionario: sus problemas, miserias y dudas no tienen nada que ver con el heroísmo necesario del que hablaba Ernesto "Che" Guevara en 1965 en la carta publicada en el periódico uruguayo *Marcha* y luego conocida como "El socialismo y el hombre en Cuba."[1]

Como en el cuento "Del rigor de la ciencia" de Jorge Luis Borges, cuyo "mapa del Imperio, tenía el tamaño del Imperio y coincidía puntualmente con él," estas narrativas intentan describir de una manera tan detallada los espacios subalternos—objetivos y subjetivos—que uno se pregunta, inocentemente tal vez, qué perdurará de ellas cuando las generaciones siguientes "las entreguen a las inclemencias del sol y de los inviernos" (Borges 225). Al mismo tiempo, en esta nueva narrativa tienen cabida sujetos subalternos que habían estado ausentes de la creación literaria cubana desde el triunfo de la Revolución; sujetos que no se acogen a las pautas sociales de compromiso político y sacrificio continuo que han definido al ser social dentro de la Revolución pero que tampoco forman parte de la oposición. Se trata de personajes que viven fuera de la sociedad, sin más ideología que la supervivencia y sin más esperanza que pasar otro día más. Son personajes que deambulan fuera de las instituciones sociales, sin oponerse a ellas, postulando nuevos usos para esos sitios, en una especie de mundo paralelo del cual no se habla públicamente a nivel oficial.

Esta literatura "mimética," por el retrato tan detallado que elabora, tiene marcados tintes naturalistas y viene funcionando como una especie de relato de viaje hacia la nada. Es también la crónica de lo que pasa en un lugar lejano—no físicamente, sino lejano para el imaginario occidental, un sitio casi impenetrable, exótico, cargado de sexualidad, rumba, ron, ruinas y miseria. Muchos escritores cubanos se han convertido así en cronistas de un lugar del que todos hablan pero al que pocos conocen de primera mano. En parte por la censura del gobierno cubano respecto a la realidad de la isla y en parte por la mala o parcial información que circula sobre Cuba en el exterior, estos escritores son los encargados de traer noticias frescas e irrefutables de lo que está pasando del otro lado de este mundo global y unipolar en que vivimos y que se llama Occidente. Paradójicamente, el lector natural de estos escritores, el cubano de la isla, es quien menos acceso ha tenido a este tipo de literatura, que parece estar respondiendo sobre todo a expectativas creadas desde el mercado internacional. En los últimos años, sin embargo, las obras de Pedro Juan Gutiérrez han comenzado a circular en Cuba, promovidas por las ferias del libro en la isla. En el caso de Antonio José Ponte, sus obras han sido publicadas principalmente en otros países como México y España y el acceso a ellas en Cuba es restringido; su circulación está limitada al préstamo entre amigos.

En este artículo intento trazar nuevos mapas de La Habana; mapas que han estado marginalizados de la historia oficial y que apenas comienzan a esbozarse en la narrativa fictícia de la nación en los últimos años. Tomando como personajes centrales a hombres y mujeres que viven fuera de la lógica del discurso político, la narrativa cubana contemporánea da cuenta de sus viajes hacia la nada, ese lugar donde el único objetivo es sobrevivir día tras día. La Habana se convierte así en una ciudad náufraga varada en medio de un mar embravecido. Las obras que analizo son: la novela *El Rey de La Habana*, de Pedro Juan Gutiérrez, publicada en Barcelona por Anagrama en 1999, y el cuento "Corazón de skitalietz," de Antonio José Ponte, perteneciente a la colección homónima que apareció en el libro *Un arte de hacer ruinas y otros cuentos*, publicado por el Fondo de Cultura Económica de México en el 2005. La colección *Corazón de skitalietz* había sido publicada antes en Cuba, en 1998.

Los personajes de ambas historias podrían ser calificados de picarescos: deambulan por la ciudad tratando de sobrevivir y en ellos prevalece la búsqueda por salvar el "yo" como único ámbito sobre el cual pueden tener propiedad. No poseen nada, sólo sus cuerpos y la constante necesidad de vivir un día más, como sea, donde sea. En su recorrido por la ciudad, estos nuevos pícaros irán narrando/creando nuevos espacios subalternos que han perdido la función para la cual fueron creados por las instituciones oficiales, ya se trate de cárceles, escuelas, viviendas, centros de trabajo, terminales de ómnibus, o incluso espacios públicos como el malecón habanero o los parques de La Habana. De este modo, los personajes de estas novelas crean y reconceptualizan los espacios a los que socialmente tienen acceso para adecuarlos a sus necesidades de supervivencia. En esta zona de negociación entre la sociedad, los espacios sociales y públicos y los personajes marginales, es donde se representa al sujeto subalterno cubano cuya capacidad de agencia es cuestionada por esta narrativa: no pueden cambiar ni poseer nada—tampoco les interesa—y su vida transcurre en el tiempo limitado de un día al siguiente. Viven sin reflexionar sobre el pasado ni hacer planes futuros; sus vidas son un presente continuo.

En sus recorridos urbanos por ambientes casi siempre marginales, peligrosos u hostiles, los personajes se van mimetizando con el espacio físico en el que interactúan hasta constituir una unidad identitaria donde al lector se le hace difícil separar o imaginar al personaje fuera de ese contexto. Hay una triple mímesis: personajes/contexto físico/sociedad. Siguiendo a Michel de Certeau, en *The Practice of Everyday Life*, la ciudad en tanto recipiente de instituciones y prácticas gubernamentales, como la policía, los hospitales, las cárceles, las escuelas y las leyes, se convierte en una maqueta que sólo desde arriba puede ser vista como una entidad unitaria. Sin embargo, para el caminante, para el pícaro moderno o *skitalietz* que la deambula, estos recorridos no obedecen a la planificación ni a los fines de estas instituciones y prácticas sociales, sino a sus propias necesidades, las cuales pueden hacer que el uso de estos sitios sea alterado, modificado o manipulado.[2] La nueva funcionalidad que adquieren los antiguos espacios sociales responde a las necesidades de supervivencia de estos seres sin esperanza. La ciudad va perdiendo su antigua coherencia funcional para permitirnos una lectura diferente, ni más ni menos real pero sí alternativa, que contradice y altera la lógica pública de sus espacios.

Según De Certeau,

> The city becomes the dominant theme in political legends, but it is no longer a field of programmed and regulated operations. Beneath the discourses that ideologize the city, the ruses and combinations of powers that have not readable identity proliferate; without points where one can take hold of them, without rational transparency, they are impossible to administer. (95)

En *El Rey de La Habana*, la relación que se establece entre Reynaldo y los diferentes espacios en los que habita es de supervivencia. En ninguno de ellos tendrá paz ni estará seguro. La azotea en la que está ubicada su casucha, es el sitio de iniciación sexual y de supervivencia económica—cría palomas con su hermano, para vendérselas a los santeros—pero es también el lugar donde pierde a su familia y la vida que hasta entonces había conocido. En el correccional perfecciona sus técnicas de supervivencia. Al escapar, comienza su viaje por una ciudad que desconoce—nunca había salido del perímetro de unas pocas cuadras alrededor de su casa—y cualquier sitio es propicio para dormitar, para esconderse y para procurarse comida, robando o mendigando: un contenedor en los muelles, una iglesia en Regla, el Cristo de Casablanca, etc. En las ruinas de Centro Habana encuentra por algún tiempo su hogar, junto a Magdalena, la vendedora de maní, pero el viaje no termina ahí, sino que prosigue, por otras casas, con otras mujeres, en otros barrios, en los alrededores del zoológico. Todos estos espacios se convierten en morada más o menos temporal, hasta que algo sucede y se ve obligado a seguir deambulando, buscando nuevos sitios en los cuales estar.

De manera similar, en "Corazón de skitalietz" los espacios van cambiando sus funciones, son inestables: Escorpión pasa algún tiempo en un hospital cuyo edificio es una antigua mansión; el instituto en el que trabajaba se va despoblando con la reubicación laboral de sus compañeros, debido a la crisis. Los apagones, tan ligados a los años noventa, convierten a la ciudad en otra, en un juego de sombras donde los personajes intentan sobrevivir como si habitaran realmente otra ciudad. Él y Veranda han abandonado sus respectivos apartamentos y se han convertido en *skitalietz*, vagabundos: "Iban en contra de los apagones, juntaban la comida conseguida. Partían el pan lo mismo que dos novios durante la guerra, uno colaba al otro en las colas. Entraban a los cines para dormir, se enseñaban lugares que siempre habían creído hermosos" (178). Mediante este proceso que De Certeau llama "la vida cotidiana," los personajes de las obras de Pedro Juan Gutiérrez y Antonio José Ponte instituyen mecanismos de supervivencia, aprovechando para ello espacios ya dados. Sin embargo, el uso que hacen estos personajes de estos espacios contradice la función para la cual fueron creados. Se establece así una discordancia entre el uso original de estos sitios y el nuevo uso que los personajes hacen de ellos.

Pese a formar parte de un grupo social más amplio, los personajes subalternos de las historias de Pedro Juan Gutiérrez y de Antonio José Ponte no conforman una comunidad—en el sentido en que Anderson habla de una comunidad imaginada, con límites específicos y diferenciada de otras—, sobre todo porque no existe una camaradería horizontal entre los miembros de estos grupos subalternos. Se trata, en todos los casos, de personajes solitarios o con mínimos intercambios con otros personajes en su misma situación. Según Pedro Juan Gutiérrez ha comentado, sus historias y personajes han sido tomados, casi literalmente, de la vida real, de su misma calle. En la contraportada de su libro se lee "una novela basada en hechos reales." Al respecto, el autor ha dicho:

> Yo camino por la calle y constantemente veo personas que podrían perfectamente ser el Rey de La Habana, personas vendiendo maní o pidiendo limosna. Es como un símbolo del pobre, el verdadero pobre que no tiene futuro y sencillamente se olvida de su futuro porque sabe que no hay futuro. Entonces lo mejor es vivir el día a día, con un

poco de ron, un cigarrito. ("El Rey de Centro Habana: Conversación")

Para ahondar aun más en la verosimilitud de su relato, el autor ha afirmado que los personajes tanto de Reynaldo como de su "mujer," Magda, la vendedora de maní, son personas reales que viven en su barrio, sólo que con otros nombres. La historia que Pedro Juan Gutiérrez nos cuenta de Reynaldo, es la de alguien que él conoce y ha sido casi transcrita a la novela. Solamente su final es ficticio, según ha afirmado el autor en la misma entrevista.

El Rey de La Habana cuenta la historia de un joven que vive al margen de la ley, de la familia y de la sociedad. Su vida se reduce a un constante desplazamiento, huyendo siempre de la policía o de otras personas. En este viaje interior por la ciudad—una ciudad que además apenas conoce y que en muchas ocasiones le es hostil—irá trazando el mapa de una Habana sucia, soez, llena de escombros y edificios a punto de derrumbarse, o en muchos casos ya derrumbados. El lenguaje que utiliza el autor es directo, simple, ordinario, de la calle, demasiado escatológico y relativo a los instintos básicos: comer, dormir, defecar, tener sexo. Casi no hay diálogos—la capacidad del personaje para producirlos o reflexionar es casi nula.

Reynaldo, llamado Rey, no tiene padre. Su familia está compuesta por su madre, que es una subnormal, su hermano y su abuela, ya muy anciana. Todos viven en un pequeño cuarto en una azotea en Centro Habana, hasta que un día, por causas ajenas a él, muere toda su familia, y aún adolescente, es llevado a un reformatorio culpado por esas muertes. Sin familia, sin raíces, sin un sitio al cual volver o donde alguien lo espere, su única ocupación y preocupación es sobrevivir. Cuando se le presenta la oportunidad de escapar del reformatorio, la aprovecha, y comienza a vagar de un lado a otro, sucio, harapiento, pobre, sin comida, sin identificación oficial, incluso sin conciencia, sin reflexionar sobre la situación en que se encuentra o cómo salir de ella. No busca explicaciones sobre su estado actual. Empieza así su vida de pícaro y también su viaje hacia la nada: sin orígenes claros, sin destino, sin familia, vive al margen de la ley—aunque no ha cometido ningún delito. Ahora es prófugo de sí mismo al carecer de identidad legal: no posee documentos que lo identifiquen. Aunque su destino es huir, nadie lo está buscando. Su principal delito a partir de entonces es no poseer una identificación oficial, y por este motivo puede ser detenido y apresado en cualquier momento. El Rey es un significante carente de significado social. Ni es "rey" ni criminal, y esta doble carencia, este vacío, es quizás su marca más peculiar y contrastante, lo que lo ubica, semántica y socialmente, en el filo de la nada.

Al escapar del reformatorio, su primera parada es la antigua azotea, y allí tiene relaciones sexuales con Fredesbinda, su antigua vecina, quien lo nombra "el Rey de La Habana" por las dimensiones de su pene, sus habilidades sexuales y las dos municiones que se había injertado en el glande mientras estaba recluido en el reformatorio. No deja de ser significativo que el apodo que le da Fredesbinda, "Rey," lleve en sí una carga irónica al informar únicamente de la capacidad sexual del personaje. Así, el diminutivo de su nombre pierde toda referencia afectiva y adquiere un nuevo significado que marcará gran parte de su proceder de ese momento en adelante. Sin embargo, el personaje jamás reflexionará sobre este asunto. Toda su historia se reduce a tener sexo con diferentes mujeres durante unos cuantos días, hasta que el hambre los hace moverse del colchón sobre el que están; pasar hambre y buscar cómo llevarse algo a la boca; drogarse con mariguana y huir, todo el tiempo huir, aunque sin rumbo fijo, sin un plan premeditado, sin ninguna estrategia.

Esta novela es la crónica de un viaje hacia la nada, pero el protagonista ni siquiera tiene la capacidad de contarla. Su acervo lingüístico es casi nulo y es además un analfabeto funcional, sin capacidad de planificación o de análisis del pasado; no puede proyectarse más allá del segundo en que vive y ni siquiera es capaz de soñar. Al respecto, ha dicho Josefina Ludmer: "el Rey es un cuerpo sexuado, sucio, animal, que vive en presente y no deja rastros ni memoria" (368). El narrador es la única posibilidad de darle voz a su historia:

> Siguió por el Malecón dos cuadras más. No sabía adónde iba. Con hambre y sin dinero. Su suerte y su desgracia es que vivía exactamente en el minuto presente. Olvidaba con precisión el minuto anterior y no se anticipaba ni un segundo al minuto próximo. Hay quien vive al día. Rey vivía al minuto. Sólo el momento exacto en que respiraba. Aquello era decisivo para sobrevivir y al mismo tiempo lo incapacitaba para proyectarse positivamente. Vivía del mismo modo que lo hace el agua estancada en un charco,

> inmovilizada, contaminada, evaporándose en medio de una
> pudrición asqueante. Y desapareciendo. (Gutiérrez 159)

La novela es narrada en tercera persona por un narrador omnisciente que suple la carencia de información del personaje. El tiempo ficcional y la historia transcurren de manera paralela hacia el futuro. Se trata de una técnica narrativa muy simple, de fácil lectura, sin grandes saltos ni complicaciones de personajes o tiempos superpuestos. La novela se puede leer prácticamente de una sentada. El lenguaje, directo y provocativo, es el lenguaje de la "calle:" soez, vulgar, cotidiano. Las oraciones, al igual que los diálogos, son breves, sin grandes subordinaciones o circunloquios. No hay muchas descripciones, ni adjetivaciones largas o complejas. Esta economía narrativa nos permite acercarnos al texto como a una fotografía en blanco y negro, precisa y directa sobre el objeto que se quiere fotografiar.

El nivel de precisión sobre lo que le interesa al autor, impide al lector echar un vistazo al resto de la sociedad, que aparece entre brumas, borrosa y sólo como algo lejanamente referencial. La técnica de focalización es aplicada sobre un tópico particular, no ya la pobreza o la marginalidad del protagonista y los otros seres con los que se relaciona, sino sobre la imposibilidad de cambiar de vida, ese presente que se vuelve eterno, donde no hay cabida para la esperanza. Esta focalización evita que el lector se distraiga en detalles o historias paralelas, y nos enfrenta de manera directa con la realidad del personaje que quiere mostrarnos. El uso llano del lenguaje le otorga a la narración una agilidad, un dinamismo paralelo al desplazamiento de Rey de un lugar a otro, su imposibilidad para estarse quieto o echar raíces en ningún sitio. Sobre la novela, Pedro Juan Gutiérrez ha dicho:

> *El Rey de La Habana* es una novela, no es un estudio socio-
> lógico ni antropológico. Pero está basada en situaciones
> que yo fui observando a lo largo de años. Los dos protago-
> nistas de la novela son personas reales: la muchacha sigue
> vendiendo maní a cuatro cuadras de aquí y el muchacho
> sigue viviendo aquí. El final, lo puse yo, claro. Pero sigue
> viviendo aquí, nosotros lo podemos ver; ahora nos aso-
> mamos a la ventana y yo te puedo decir, "Mira, ése es el
> protagonista de *El Rey de La Habana.*" Y son analfabetos,
> dejaron la escuela cuando tenían 5 ó 6 años, y la madre es

mongólica. Son unos casos muy particulares. Vamos a ver
esto claro, yo en ningún modo estoy hablando de toda la
juventud cubana ni pretendo hacer un análisis sociológico
de la juventud cubana. Es una novela con ciertos personajes
determinados. ("El Rey de Centro Habana. Conversación")

Los personajes de la novela, según afirma el propio Gutiérrez, forman
parte de una realidad que simbólicamente ha perdido su homoge-
neidad debido a la crisis económica y al desgaste de un discurso
ideológico que no se logra sostener en lo cotidiano. En esta nueva
realidad el ideal del "hombre nuevo" ha desaparecido, y en su lugar
han aflorado seres de todo tipo cuyo único objetivo es sobrevivir, pasar
de un día al siguiente. Como bien aclara Gutiérrez, sus personajes no
son el retrato de toda la sociedad cubana, aunque sí representan a un
segmento cuya presencia queda al margen del reconocimiento oficial.

Antonio José Ponte, por su parte, ha descrito así el escenario
en el que se construyen sus historias: "en Cuba no ha existido una
guerra pero es una ciudad que parece haber pasado una guerra. Tener
que habitar las ruinas, habitar en una ciudad ruinosa, casas ruinosas,
ambiente ruinoso, todo eso te da un tono que no te va a abandonar
nunca" (Serna y Solano 131-132). De ahí que en "Corazón de skitalietz," Antonio José Ponte dé vida a personajes que viven en la calle,
sin casa ni sitio fijo: los *skitalietz* o vagabundos, a quienes el poder
les niega incluso la libertad de no tener, voluntariamente, un hogar; a
quienes se acusa de querer tener la ciudad completa para ellos, como
casa infinita. En éste, como en su cuento "Un arte de hacer ruinas,"
Ponte representa una doble imposibilidad convertida en milagro:
que la ciudad siga en pie, contra todo pronóstico de la arquitectura,
y que sus habitantes, atravesados por la locura y el desamparo,
sobrevivan y encuentren motivos para mantener la fe. Tanto en la
novela de Pedro Juan Gutiérrez como en el cuento de Antonio José
Ponte los personajes son testigos sobrevivientes de una ciudad que se
cae a pedazos, pero cuya ruina no es tema del discurso oficial. "Las
ruinas de La Habana, concentradas mayormente en el municipio de
Centro Habana, datan del siglo XIX, así como algunas mansiones
de principios del siglo XX en el Vedado y otras barriadas habaneras.
El estado ruinoso no lo da la antigüedad, sino el abandono que han
sufrido durante las últimas cuatro décadas" (Puñales-Alpízar, "La
Habana (im)posible").

"¿A qué acude la gente para seguir con vida?" (*Corazón* 158). ¿Qué impulsa a los personajes de estas historias a seguir buscando un motivo para vivir? Esta pregunta, que en algún momento le hace el gato de Veranda a Escorpión en "Corazón de skitalietz" es una cuestión de fondo que une las narrativas de Ponte y de Gutiérrez: qué hace que la gente siga viviendo en situaciones extremas, qué hace que los edificios sigan en pie, pese a la certeza científica de su caída, pese a la hostilidad con que la ciudad los trata. En ambas obras, los personajes son una alegoría—directa, en el caso de *El Rey de La Habana*; indirecta en "Corazón de skitalietz"—del desamparo socioeconómico e ideológico en que quedaron los cubanos tras el fin del socialismo soviético y el inicio de lo que Fidel Castro denominó "período especial en tiempos de paz."[3] Los personajes de las dos novelas moldearán sus vidas a partir de la crisis económica y social que trajeron consigo estos cambios drásticos. Al referirse al proceso de creación de *Trilogía sucia de La Habana* Pedro Juan Gutiérrez comentó:[4]

> En aquel momento, yo era un tipo lleno de ira, de confusiones . . . Y no sólo yo, creo que toda mi generación. Date cuenta que la generación mía se dedicó al proyecto revolucionario en cuerpo y alma. Y a partir del 90 todo se empieza a convertir en sal y agua, los que lo vivimos recordamos el hambre que se pasó en Cuba. . . [...] En el 94 empecé a escribir *Trilogía sucia* con muchísima furia, muy defraudado, molesto, era casi un acto de venganza. Contra mí mismo y contra todo . . . . ("Diálogo con Pedro Juan Gutiérrez")

Esta rabia de la que habla Pedro Juan Gutiérrez encuentra su representación en la apatía de los personajes de "Corazón de skitalietz" y en la sordidez con que viven los de *El Rey de La Habana*. En ninguno de los dos casos puede obviarse el impacto de la crisis económica en todos los ámbitos de la vida de los personajes: todos han perdido algo. La novela de Gutiérrez da cuenta de estas pérdidas desde la primera línea: "Aquel pedazo de azotea era el más puerco del edificio. Cuando comenzó la crisis en 1990 ella perdió su trabajo de limpiapisos" (9). A partir de esta pérdida inicial que sufre la madre de Reynaldo, se irán acumulando otras pérdidas durante el resto de la narración.

En el caso de "Corazón de skitalietz" las pérdidas también marcan el destino de los personajes. A diferencia de Rey, que es sacado de su hogar y se ve obligado a merodear de un sitio a otro para sobrevivir, el personaje de Ponte es un historiador que se queda sin trabajo repentinamente. Sus años de investigaciones, de artículos y libros publicados se esfuman, dejan de contar. No pierde su hogar, pero ya no tiene nada que lo sostenga—ni intelectual ni económicamente—y decide echarse a la calle, donde encuentra a otras personas que como él, han sufrido diferentes pérdidas y buscan, deambulando la ciudad, algo que les devuelva un poco la fe, las esperanzas. "Tantos avisos de gente desaparecida y él sin haberse dado cuenta. Afuera, fuera de la mansión devenida en hospital de día, la ciudad estaba llena de skitalietz, gente que vagabundea aparentemente sin destino" (Ponte, *Un arte* 165). Pese a que los personajes de ambas historias viven en una ciudad populosa como La Habana—que tiene más de dos millones y medio de habitantes—, son seres solitarios en un medio adverso en el que nunca están a salvo por completo. Siempre puede haber alguien que los persiga, los denuncie o los encarcele, que los lleve a un hospital de locos, los clasifique o los convierta en una estadística. Los gestos de amistad, humanidad o solidaridad son escasos, casi inexistentes. La ciudad es, además, un sitio del que no se puede escapar: "la maldita circunstancia del agua por todas partes"—como diría Virgilio Piñera en "La isla en peso"—los detiene junto al Malecón, ese espacio que en las dos historias se convierte en lugar de intercambio, de transacciones de todo tipo, pero sobre todo, de supervivencia.[5]

En esa ciudad por la que deambulan, no existe una geografía urbana que establezca claramente del todo las fronteras entre los diferentes mundos que conviven en ella. La Habana finisecular en la que viven los personajes combina en un mismo territorio edificios que se derrumban impasiblemente con sitios de mejor suerte económica y arquitectónica. En ciertos barrios, en una misma calle, pueden convivir espacios míseros y espacios prósperos en un raro equilibrio que desafía cualquier postulado sobre la delimitación entre pobreza y prosperidad, entre violencia socio-arquitectónica y áreas de seguridad. Los personajes de las obras de Ponte y de Gutiérrez, sin embargo, no ocupan ninguna de estas dos geografías. Son invisibles para ambas y su deambular entre la una y la otra pasa desapercibido la mayor parte de las veces. Son seres transparentes en los cuales nadie repara. Su falta de agencia y su desvinculación total con cualquier tipo de institución o agrupación los convierte en entes inexistentes a los ojos de la sociedad.

"Me gustaría vivir en una ciudad como ésta, me encantaría quedarme en ella," (156) afirma Escorpión, personaje principal de "Corazón de skitalietz." Para él, la ciudad es un sitio imaginado, que no coincide con el real: "La ciudad vista desde el hotel y la que había caminado hasta el mar con Veranda estarían ahora en otra parte, no podía ser ésta. Existía entre ellas la misma diferencia que entre una pesadilla y una narración de esa pesadilla al día siguiente, cuando ya todo parecía inofensivo" (174). ¿Cuál es la ciudad real? ¿La que se extiende frente a los personajes o la que van creando ellos en su deambular, en su diario sobrevivir? Pese a que el espacio público tiene una materialidad física, ésta sólo adquiere valor cuando se convierte en un lugar de interrelaciones, en este caso, subalternas. Según Michel de Certeau,

> [t]he space of a tactic is the space of the other. Thus it must play on and with a terrain imposed on it and organized by the law of a foreign power . . . it's a maneuver 'within the enemy's field of vision,' and within enemy territory. It does not, therefore, have the options of planning general strategy and viewing the adversary as a whole within a distinct, visible, and objectifiable space. It operates in isolated actions, blow by blow. It takes advantage of "opportunities" and depends on them. . . . What it wins it cannot keep. . . . A tactic is an art of the weak . . . it is determined by the absence of power. (37)

Los personajes de las dos historias no tienen poder ni control sobre las situaciones en las que se encuentran; sólo pueden acomodarse y tomar las ventajas que cada momento o sitio les ofrecen.

En ambas historias, es la memoria la que otorga un sentido a estos espacios públicos. Los personajes se sienten ligados a ellos por lo que, a nivel personal, les ha pasado ahí: el fin de la inocencia y el lanzamiento al desamparo, en el caso del Rey; y el apego, el afecto a las ruinas, en el caso de Escorpión, quien piensa:

> Caminaba por una película de guerra. No se escuchaban las alarmas, nadie esperaba ataques del enemigo. Todo parecía haber sucedido ya, todas las devastaciones. . . . Donde antes se levantaba un edificio, habían construido

un basurero. . . . Fuera del instituto, . . . le quedaba aún la
ciudad, esas ruinas por las que atravesaba. Eran su abrigo,
no podría alejarse. (*Corazón* 168-169)

Los personajes de Gutiérrez, Rey y Magda, por su parte, son testigos
presenciales, y sobrevivientes, de cómo la ciudad se va convirtiendo
en una gran ruina, cómo los edificios se derrumban y en su lugar
sólo quedan escombros amontonados de donde sólo queda escapar.
El edificio donde vivía Magda se viene abajo, y ellos sobreviven
milagrosamente:

Un estruendo enorme y todo se precipitó abajo. El techo
y los muros. El piso cedió también y todo siguió cinco
metros más, hasta el suelo. . . . Huyeron hacia la calle. . . .
Uno gritó: ¡Mira, quedaron dos vivos! Ellos no miraron
atrás. . . . A sus espaldas resonó un estruendo: el último
trozo de la habitación de Magda también se vino al piso.
(*El Rey* 202-203)

En ambos casos, los personajes están ligados a las ruinas, han convi-
vido con ellas, e incluso, han logrado sobrevivir a los derrumbes. Ante
sus ojos la ciudad se va destruyendo, perdiendo corporeidad y esta
pérdida física de alguna manera es la alegoría de pérdidas mucho más
profundas y vitales que van sufriendo los personajes en el transcurso
de ambas historias. Escorpión y Veranda, en la noveleta de Ponte,
toman pastillas para dormir y no tener que lidiar con estas pérdidas
ni con la realidad de los otros, de la ciudad, y de las instituciones en
las que no son aceptados. Por su parte, Rey y Magda pasan la mayor
parte del tiempo bebiendo alcohol, preocupados por el hambre sólo
cuando la sienten, tratando de sobrevivir a los edificios que se caen, a
la sociedad que los margina. Para todos ellos la única posibilidad de
escapar es construir su propia realidad: en los sueños, en la inconscien-
cia etílica. En ambos casos, la ciudad se ha convertido en la metáfora
de una nación de la que no forman parte oficialmente, pero de la cual
no es posible huir.

Aunque existen marcadas diferencias entre los personajes y las
historias de estos autores, tanto sus vidas como sus muertes—en el
caso de Magda, Rey y Veranda—pasan desapercibidas por el resto de
la sociedad y sus instituciones. Nadie los va a echar de menos, nadie

los va a recordar. Con ellos se acaba su mundo, no dejan, como afirma Josefina Ludmer, "ni rastro ni memoria" (368). Estos personajes viven en un presente continuo, fuera de la sociedad, sin familia, sin amigos, sin recordar el pasado ni planificar el futuro, dos ámbitos temporales sobre los cuales no tienen ningún control. La ciudad, que les fue hostil siempre, se los traga, los engulle, sin darles posibilidad alguna de cambiar su situación, de construirse un mañana. Aislados, sin mayor intercambio humano real con otros, la vida de estos personajes transcurre en espacios subalternos y marginalizados que, pese a no formar parte del discurso hegemónico que construye una imagen de nación desde el poder, sí conforman una geografía heterogénea dentro del amplio espectro de la realidad cubana actual.

Notas

1. Según Ernesto "Che" Guevara, el "hombre nuevo" debía tener dos cualidades principales: por una parte, tendría la virtud de haber nacido ya sin el "pecado original," es decir, fuera del seno de la burguesía, y por otra debía ser educado en el espíritu permanente de sacrificio y heroísmo que le permitiera enfrentar la cotidianeidad con la misma entrega que la ciudadanía se había movilizado durante los grandes hechos de los primeros años revolucionarios, como la Crisis de Octubre, en 1962 o el ciclón Flora, en 1964: "encontrar la fórmula para perpetuar en la vida cotidiana esa actitud heroica, es una de nuestras tareas fundamentales desde el punto de vista ideológico." Véase: "El socialismo y el hombre en Cuba."

2. *Skitalietz* es una transcripción fonética de la palabra que en ruso significa 'vagabundo.'

3. Fidel Castro anunció el "período especial en tiempos de paz" durante el V Congreso de la Federación de Mujeres Cubanas, FMC, el 10 de marzo de 1990. En términos generales Cuba literalmente perdió más del 80% de su intercambio mercantil.

4. *Trilogía sucia de La Habana* (1998) está compuesta por los libros de cuentos "Anclado en tierra de nadie," "Nada que hacer" y "Sabor a mí."

5. Así comienza el poema de Piñera, escrito en 1943.

Obras citadas

Anderson, Benedict. *Imagined Communities*. London: Verso, 2003. Print.

Borges, Jorge Luis. *Obras completas*. Tomo 2. Buenos Aires: Emecé Editores, 1974. Print.

Certeau, Michel de. *The Practice of Everyday Life*. Berkeley: University of California Press, 1988. Print.

——. *The Writing of History*. New York: Columbia University Press, 1988. Print.

Guevara, Ernesto "Che." "El socialismo y el hombre en Cuba." *Patria Grande*. Web. 2 March, 2010.

Gutiérrez, Pedro Juan. *El Rey de La Habana*. Barcelona: Anagrama, 1999. Print.

——. Entrevista de Rafael Grillo. "Diálogo con Pedro Juan Gutiérrez. Cita en la azotea del Rey de La Habana (I)." *Isliada.com. Literatura cubana contemporánea*. Web. 16 Feb. 2012.

——. Entrevista de Stephen J Clark. "El Rey de Centro Habana. Conversación con Pedro Juan Gutiérrez." *Todo sobre Pedro Juan. Sitio oficial del escritor cubano Pedro Juan Gutiérrez*. Web. 10 Oct. 2011.

Ludmer, Josefina. "Ficciones cubanas de los últimos años: el problema de la literatura política." *Cuba: un siglo de literatura (1902-2002)*. Eds. Anke Birkenmaier y Roberto González Echeverría. Madrid: Editorial Colibrí, 2004. 357-371. Print.

Ponte, Antonio José. *Cuentos de todas partes del imperio*. Francia: Editions Deleatur, 2000. Print.

——. Entrevista personal. 28 noviembre, 2005 (email). Inédita.

——. Entrevista de Mercedes Serna y Anna Solana. "Entrevista a Antonio José Ponte." *Cuadernos hispanoamericanos* 665 (Noviembre 2005): 127-134. Print

——. *Un arte de hacer ruinas y otros cuentos*. Ciudad de México: Fondo de Cultura Económica, 2005. Print.

——. *Un seguidor de Montaigne mira La Habana. Las comidas profundas*. Madrid: Verbum, 2001. Print.

Puñales-Alpízar, Damaris. "La Habana (im)posible de Ponte o las ruinas de una ciudad atravesada por una guerra que nunca tuvo lugar." *Ciberletras. Revista de crítica literaria y de cultura* 20 (Dic. 2008). Web. 14 Feb. 2012.

"Tratar de decir lo que la gente no quiere oír." Una entrevista a Pedro Juan Gutiérrez

Jamie Fudacz
University of California, Los Angeles

Nacido en 1950 en Matanzas, Cuba, Pedro Juan Gutiérrez es periodista, poeta, escritor y pintor. Entre 1998 y 2003, la casa editora Anagrama publicó sus obras más reconocidas. Éstas forman parte del llamado "Ciclo de Centro Habana" e incluyen *Trilogía sucia de La Habana, El Rey de La Habana, Animal Tropical, El insaciable hombre araña* y *Carne de perro*. La escritura de Pedro Juan Gutiérrez se destaca por representar la vida cotidiana de los habitantes indigentes de Centro Habana y su lucha por sobrevivir en medio de la crisis económica que sufrió el país en los años noventa. La centralidad de personajes marginales en combinación con un estilo sencillo y un lenguaje visceral ha motivado a la crítica a comparar su escritura con la de llamados realistas sucios: Henry Miller, Charles Bukowski y Raymond Carver. Ganador del Premio Alfonso García-Ramos en el 2000 por su novela *Animal tropical*, el autor divide hoy en día su tiempo entre Centro Habana y Canarias.

Esta entrevista tuvo lugar en febrero del 2011, en la Unión de Escritores y Artistas de Cuba en El Vedado, La Habana.

Mester: Has dicho que tus obras están dentro de una línea muy fuerte del realismo sucio. ¿Cómo defines al realismo sucio? ¿Es un género? ¿Un subgénero?

Pedro Juan Gutiérrez: Mira, lo que sucede es lo siguiente. Yo incluso estuve leyendo una entrevista a Richards Ford y en esa entrevista que se publicó en España, en español por supuesto, Richard Ford aclara sobre el realismo sucio. Dice que el realismo sucio fue inventado. Este término fue inventado por unos editores que en algún momento quisieron provocar una atención sobre Raymond Carver, sobre él, y sobre otros autores. Lo que pasa es que nada más que han sobrevivido como punto de interés Raymond Carver y Richard Ford. Después conmigo pasó lo mismo. Anagrama que es quien publica mis libros en Barcelona, publicaba, publica a Bukowski, publica a Raymond Carver y publica a Richard Ford.

M: ¿Y, entonces?

PJG: Entonces todo es un truco comercial de la editorial. Es decir, "El realismo sucio de Pedro Juan Gutiérrez," "El realista sucio del Caribe," "El Bukowski del Caribe," o qué sé yo, "del trópico," "El Henry Miller tropical," todas esas cosas. Entonces es más bien un reclamo de tipo comercial que otra cosa, ¿no? Porque si tú vas a ver desde un punto de vista ético qué cosa es sucio y qué cosa es limpio es que mis personajes pueden ser gente muy vulgar, gente de los bajos fondos, un poco delincuente, un poco. ¿Pero son más sucios que un Viceministro que quizás está de traje y corbata pero es un tipo corrupto que está robando? ¿Entonces cuál de los dos es más sucio? ¿Aquella prostituta que está en Centro Habana, o el Viceministro que está de traje y corbata, en un Mercedes Benz, o en un BMW robando millones de dólares al estado? Lo mismo aquí que en México, que en España, que en donde sea. Entonces, eso de suciedad y limpieza es muy relativo, ¿no? Tiene que ver mucho con las apariencias. Yo por lo menos lo veo así. Por eso, a mí no me interesa mucho la terminología esa del realismo sucio. Yo sé que yo soy un escritor realista desde el punto de vista de que me baso en la realidad, pero yo creo que todo el mundo se basa en la realidad. ¿Porque tú, qué vas a inventar? A partir de las cosas que estás observando es que puedes escribir. Entonces en ese sentido soy realista, pero ya después sucio o limpio, ya.

M: ¿Pero no podemos verlo de una manera más estética que ética? O sea, tiene algo que ver con tener que mirar toda la realidad. Muchos autores son realistas, pero sus lectores no tienen que leer sobre las cosas más íntimas de las vidas de sus personajes: de lo sexual, lo esca-tológico, lo violento. Para mí, esto es algo que define el género del realismo sucio. Para los lectores puede ser un poco incómodo porque tienen que ver las cosas que no quieren ver. La suciedad puede surgir de las descripciones gráficas de esos aspectos no tan bonitos de la vida humana más que de la posición marginal de los personajes.

PJG: Mira, ahí sí vas muy atinada. Tú me acabas de decir una cosa que es la esencia de la posición estética mía. Es decir, tratar de decir lo que la gente no quiere oír, lo que la gente no quiere ver. Yo durante, ya te dije, durante 26 años fui periodista. Un periodista tiene que manipular mucho la información. Da igual si es en Cuba; sí aquí es mucho, aquí es mucho lo que hay que manipular la información. Pero es igual si es en Estados Unidos, si es en China, o si vives en España o donde sea. Tienes que escribir de acuerdo a los intereses del periódico para el que tú trabajas o la agencia de noticias, o lo que sea. Entonces, Cuba ha tenido un proceso político basado en el heroísmo. Somos heroicos. Estados Unidos nos está atacando. Somos heroicos. Somos heroicos. Somos heroicos. Llega un momento en que yo estoy ya hasta los cojones del heroísmo. Estoy hasta los cojones de grandeza, de dignidad de la patria, la moral de la patria, la dignidad de los cubanos. Entonces casi que inconscientemente yo reacciono al otro extremo. En vez de tanto patriotismo y tanto heroísmo, y tanto, y tanta obra de teatro politiquera, pues esencialmente yo reacciono todo lo contrario. Y entonces, pues me fijo donde los escritores normalmente no habían fijado nunca la vista. Por una simple razón. Los escritores normalmente viven aquí. Son de la clase media. Viven en el Vedado. Viven en Miramar. Viven un poquito apartado. Tienen una profesión. ¿Tú te das cuenta? Y yo estaba viviendo en una situación muy difícil en Centro Habana. Es decir, en un edificio arruinado, completamente arruinado. Mi casa cayéndose el techo, que tuvo muchos años con el techo cayéndose que me iba a quedar sin casa. No había comida por toda la crisis económica. Entonces, no había comida. No tenía dinero. El dinero que ganaba como periodista no me alcanzaba para nada. El salario mío como periodista equivalía a treinta huevos. Treinta huevos, sí. No había huevos, pero si yo conseguía huevos, y compraba treinta huevos, se acababa el salario mío del mes. Esa era la situación que yo tenía que enfrentar en el 1991, 1992, 1993, hasta que en el año 1994 ya estoy hasta los cojones de esa situación tan degradante. Yo me alcoholicé mucho como una salida a la situación, me alcoholizaba mucho y me puse muy curioso, muy depravado con muchas mujeres. Era como una salida. Era como una manera de no pensar en los problemas que tenía. Estaba viviendo solo en una casa que se me estaba cayendo a pedazos encima. Sin dinero para reparar la casa. Sin dinero para comer. Y entonces, me pongo a escribir de eso. Pero incluso no era un proyecto intelectual como este que tú estás pensando muy lógicamente, con raciocinio. Estás organizando las cosas. Una novela uno la tiene que organizar de esa manera, con cierto grado de raciocinio. Vas dejando la poesía, vas dejando el misterio, pero tiene que haber un orden. Bueno, *Trilogía sucia* yo no lo organicé nunca de esa manera. Por eso son pequeños textos corticos de siete páginas, ocho páginas, tres páginas, que se van organizando como un mural de las cosas que pasan. Por eso hay quien dice que es una novela y hay quien dice que no, que es un libro de cuentos, que son sesenta cuentos. Para mí eran cuentos. Pero inconscientemente yo estaba como dejando constancia de una situación que nadie la había reflejado hasta ese momento como literatura, como un contexto literario. Date cuenta de más; de que aquí en Cuba hay una larga tradición de literatura barroca. Alejo Carpentier y Lezama Lima. O Virgilio Piñera. O, hay muchos escritores. Es una gran literatura utilizando el idioma de una manera extraordinaria, de una manera intensa. Yo, que el español es mi idioma original, me era muy difícil, me es hoy en día difícil leer a Lezama Lima. Y a Alejo Carpentier tenía que leerlo con diccionario. Hoy en día es que yo logro leer a Alejo Carpentier con más fluidez. Hace ahora poco tiempo. Pero cuando yo tenía veinte años me era casi imposible leer a Alejo Carpentier. Entonces es un país de una gran tradición barroca. Un idioma que se presta para todo ese barroquismo porque es un idioma muy complicado gramaticalmente, pero que además tiene una enorme cantidad de palabras. El diccionario de la Academia de la Lengua es una cosa gigantesca, una Biblia. Es enorme. Un idioma muy enriquecido. Y de pronto yo cierro mucho a un close-up, como muy cerquita. Digo, mira a mí lo que me interesa es esto y un lenguaje mínimo, y lo voy a expresar todo con unas estructuras gramaticales muy simples, pero esto lo hago inconscientemente, como una reacción a toda aquella gran pompa, a todo aquel gran heroísmo, aquel patriotismo, a todas aquellas cosas que ya me tenían cansado. Por ahí van las cosas, más o menos.

M: Entiendo el poder que estos cuentos pueden tener para los habitantes de Centro Habana, de poder ver sus propias vidas en el libro. Pero en el extranjero, como tienes tantos lectores internacionales, qué visión de Cuba quieres que ellos saquen del libro. ¿Qué visión de Cuba dejas con ellos? Hay unos críticos que dicen que toda esa literatura de la violencia es la única cosa que los lectores fuera de América Latina, fuera del Caribe, conocen. Y que puede ser otra forma de exotismo. Que antes todo era realismo mágico y ahora todo es realismo sucio, y violencia, y narcotráfico. Entonces, ¿qué quieres que tus lectores en otros países piensen de Cuba?

PJG: Mira, lo que un escritor quiere, o desea, o intenta expresar a la larga tiene poca importancia, o ninguna importancia, porque cada lector hace su propia lectura. Si a ti te interesa el Caribe, Cuba, Jamaica, o lo que sea, tú tratas de viajar a ese país y tratas de formar tu propia opinión. A mí hay quien me dice eso, me dice, "bueno pero es que tus libros son muy negativos, porque los leen extranjeros y pensarán que todos los Cubanos somos así," y mira, hay que ser muy estúpido para pensar eso, porque es como pensar que en la época de Homero todos los griegos eran como Ulises. Todos los griegos no eran Ulises. Que tú me digas que todos los griegos eran como los esclavos que iban remando la barca de Ulises, bueno ya eso es más aceptable, pero como Ulises, ¡no! Es un protagonista, una figura, una construcción literaria, que es lo que hago yo; una construcción literaria utilizando fragmentos de la realidad, pedacitos de la realidad. Pero que no quiere decir que ahora hay muchas Cubas, como hay muchos Estados Unidos, como hay muchas Españas. No es lo mismo la España del norte como la del sur, que los catalanes, que en Canarias. Son diferentes formas de ver el mundo. Con esto pasa lo mismo. A la larga cada lector hace su propia lectura, al extremo de que hay investigadores así como tú que creen que yo lo que hago es antropología. Hay una antropóloga de la Universidad de Chicago que está convencida de que yo lo que hago es estudios antropológicos. Hay quien cree que es periodismo, que no tiene mayor importancia, no tiene mayor transcendencia como literatura, que es simple periodismo de la época de la crisis económica fuerte. ¡Qué sé yo qué! Hay quien cree que son unas memorias de un periodo especial, un periodo determinado. Cada cual hace su lectura como le conviene, como le interesa. Eso es por un lado. Pero por el otro lado los lectores cubanos tienen mínimo acceso a mis libros. Mis libros casi no se publican aquí. Se han publicados muy pocos. Se ha publicado *Animal tropical* en ediciones pequeñitas de dos mil ejemplares que desaparecen así. Se desaparecen en un segundo. Es como si fuera pornografía. Aquí que está prohibida la pornografía, es como si fuera pornografía. *Animal tropical, Melancolía de los leones, Nuestro GG en La Habana* y *El Rey de La Habana* que acaba de salir ahora. Esos cuatro, esos cuatro libros son los que se han publicado, te repito, en ediciones pequeñitas de dos mil ejemplares que nadie los consigue.

M: Para cambiar de tema, me interesa mucho el rol de la ciudad dentro de tus ficciones. ¿Puedes hablar un poquito de cómo conceptualizas a La Habana? ¿Cómo es la interacción entre la ciudad y los personajes?

PJG: No sé. Es dificilísimo explicar eso así de esa manera. Yo siempre he vivido en ciudades. Así, yo no soy un hombre de campo. El campo me gusta un rato, dos o tres días, pero no. En todo caso me gusta el mar. Vivir cerca del mar, siempre he vivido cerca del mar pero en ciudades, Matanzas, aquí en La Habana. Porque en la ciudad hay mucho conflicto, mucho antagonismo. Y es la esencia del asunto. Por lo menos para mí la literatura es conflicto y es antagonismo. Si no hay conflicto, no hay antagonismo, no hay problemas, pues la dramaturgia no puede avanzar. Hay otros escritores, escritores alemanes contemporáneos por ejemplo, que son más aburridos, y entonces hay a veces un solo personaje. Hay uno que se llama Sebald. Es dificilísimo de leer porque es él solo prácticamente con su mente haciendo recorridos por Europa, por Italia, por ahí, por allá. Pero es como él solo, un tipo como que está como medio loco, muy tímido, no sé. Entonces, no hay nada, no. Todo es . . . si tiene sexo con alguien, pues, no lo dice. Dice, no, "me fui, caminamos por un parque de noche," y qué sé yo qué. Y no regresábamos y ya. Bueno "en Venecia salí con un muchacho en una lancha," pero parece como un poco homosexual también. "Salimos en una lancha y vimos las estrellas," y qué sé yo qué, y "regresamos y," no sé, no cuenta nada. Yo no concibo la literatura de esa manera. Es decir, a mí me gusta que haya conflicto, que haya antagonismo, que haya problemas, que haya sexo, que haya lo que tiene que haber. Y eso es más fácil en las ciudades, ¿no? Da igual si es La Habana o si es Río de Janeiro. Hay ciudades que son muy complicadas, que son muy conflictivas. Por lo regular en las zonas de mayor pobreza. Por ejemplo en Madrid, en el centro de Madrid hay una zona que se llama La Latina. Toda esa zona es interesantísima porque es muy fuerte. Viven gitanos. Vive gente pobre, viejos jubilados que se roban cosas en el supermercado y las venden allí en la boca del metro. Tú los ves vendiendo paqueticos de chorizo, de aceitunas, cualquier cosa, latas de atún. No sé que pensaba hasta que me dijeron no, que son jubilados que ganan muy poco. Van al supermercado, roban, y entonces venden aquí. Es en el centro de Madrid. Y en Río de Janeiro también. Yo he estado muchas veces en Brasil, en São Paolo. São Paolo ni qué decir, São Paolo que es la gran locura. Ciudad México, que he estado unas veces en Ciudad de México y es una gran locura. Yo podría escribir perfectamente si conociera esas ciudades, ¿no?, en vez de La Habana.

M: Me parece que, dentro de La Habana que describes en tus obras, la división entre los espacios públicos y los espacios privados casi no existe. Muchos han hablado del voyeurismo como un tema de importancia en tus ficciones, pero también existe un exhibicionismo fuerte y preponderante. ¿Estás de acuerdo? ¿De dónde viene esa necesidad de mostrarse, de ver y ser visto?

PJG: Tienes que buscar un psicólogo para que me analice. No, en general el cubano, más bien el habanero joven, sobre todo si está bien dotado, pues es muy exhibicionista. No es que todo el mundo sea así. Pero eso pasa un poco también con los brasileños. Las mujeres y los hombres cuando son jóvenes, tienen un cuerpo muy bonito, y entonces les gusta exhibirse. Al extremo de en los carnavales de Río las mujeres salen con los pechos al aire y les encanta exhibir sus pechos. Lo ven de una manera muy natural. Y aquí en las playas tú puedes ver que los hombres que están bien dotados usan trusas bañadores pequeños para que se les marque el paquete como dicen en España, no. Que es una forma de exhibicionismo también, ¿no? Entonces van de lo más orondo con su machismo. Hay una mezcla ahí de machismo con cuerpos hermosos. Porque realmente por nuestro mestizaje entre negros y españoles, europeos, pues creo que es lo mismo que pasa en Brasil, ¿no? Pues realmente somos de una estatura, somos bonitos, casi siempre los hombres están bien dotados, las mujeres también están bien dotadas. Y entonces, hay ahí un poco de orgullo, y se ve de manera. Es la latinidad. Pero los italianos también son un poco así. Son más todavía. Yo pienso que es una mezcla del temperamento latino con la cosa aquí caribeña, del calor, del machismo. Hay una mezcla que nos hace ser un poco exhibicionistas. Somos muy sexuales. Y te repito que yo, en ese deseo de fijar la vista en contextos que no habían sido llevados a la literatura hasta este momento, hay quien dice incluso que la literatura cubana es una antes de *Trilogía sucia de La Habana* y otra después de *Trilogía sucia*, que *Trilogía sucia* marca un punto. No sé si será así o no. Al extremo de aquí *Trilogía sucia* no se publica. Ni se va a publicar en muchísimos años. Así que evidentemente molesta, ¿no? Es un libro que molesta. Cuando un libro molesta tanto, por algo será. Yo me alegro de que no se publique, porque evidentemente es un libro que está marcando y que está originando polémica y envidia. Y que tiene cierto poder porque, evidentemente le tienen miedo, ¿no? Cuando no tienen miedo pues publican y ya, pasó. Pero evidentemente los editores tienen miedo de publicarlo.

M: Como escribes sobre la lucha por sobrevivir durante la crisis económica, muchos críticos han comentado acerca del fuerte individualismo que existe en ese contexto. ¿Crees que existe cierta forma de solidaridad o de comunión? Estoy pensando en el cuento "Plenilunio en la azotea," cuando todos los vecinos enfrentan juntos a la policía para apoyar a Pedro Juan. ¿Hay la posibilidad de sentirse parte de una comunidad o formar una comunidad bajo estas circunstancias?

PJG: Sí, de hecho sí la hay; siempre contra el poder. Es decir si tú vives, es que obviamente tú nunca has vivido en situaciones así, pero es igual, si tú eres pobre y vives en un lugar, un solar, una cuartería donde hay gente muy pobre que está siempre al margen de la ley, porque uno está vendiendo drogas, el otro está vendiendo aparaticos robados de la tienda, el otro está vendiendo cosas robadas, cadenas de oro, lo que sea, el otro está vendiendo sexo, porque es un negro y tiene un rabo largo así entonces está enseñando el sexo a las doce de la noche. Así que todo el mundo está fuera de la ley. Y entonces hay una unión inconsciente contra la policía cualquiera que . . . "¡oye qué tú vienes a hacer aquí, ahh!" para alejar a la policía. Meterle miedo a la policía y que no entre al lugar. Aquí en La Habana en algunos barrios la policía no entra sola. Eso se lleva a un extremo ya en las favelas de Brasil, que la policía no puede entrar. La policía cuando entra es disparando porque es muy cerrado. Así que se crea esa solidaridad, sí. Entre gentes que son muy marginales y que tienen que defenderse. Pero no hay otro tipo. Después, entre ellos mismos hay mucha violencia.

M: ¿Y piensas que esta solidaridad que existe entre las personas al margen de la ley puede ser una manera de formar comunidades que no tienen nada que ver con el estado y sus instituciones?

PJG: ¡Totalmente! ¡Sí, sí, totalmente! Todo el que . . . todas las prostitutas, son outsiders. Completamente. Son gentes que están fuera del sistema; que no les interesa. Yo cuando llegué a Centro Habana, yo no soy de Centro Habana por supuesto. Yo era periodista. Pertenecía a la clase media. Tenía carro. Viajaba al exterior una o dos veces al año. Llego a Centro Habana en el año 1988. Yo tenía treinta y ocho años, y yo como que vivía en este mundo, en un mundo de intelectuales, de escritores, de periodistas, de universidades y otra cosa. Y de pronto llego allí y cuando ya empiezo a convivir en el barrio, tenía que ir a la bodega a comprar comida o a la placita a comprar las viandas, convivir allí, me doy cuenta de que a esa gente como que no le interesaba nada de la Revolución ni la política. No es que la rechazaran y dijeran "¡Ay, esto es malo!" No, ni siquiera eso. Sino sencillamente ellos vivían encerrados en su pequeño mundo porque tienen que buscar un dólar para vivir hoy, y mañana igual. Y pasaba lo que pasaba. Entonces, sencillamente no es que estén en contra del sistema, sea el sistema que sea, capitalismo, soc . . . no, no, no, es que están dentro de su propio sistema. Por eso en mayor o menor medida todo el mundo funcionaba allí en aquel barrio. Estoy hablando del año 1988, 1989, antes de que comenzara la crisis económica que comienza en sí ya en el año 1990-91. Y en el 1992 ya era hambre total y la miseria total, y no había nada. Y Centro Habana, el centro de la ciudad, sufrió mucho el embate de esa crisis económica porque la gente quedó muy abandonada a su suerte, ¿no? Hubo muchas cosas que yo no las escribí en la *Trilogía sucia*. Yo me enteraba porque yo seguía trabajando como periodista. Y yo me enteraba de muchas cosas que yo ni siquiera las utilizaba porque eran demasiado. Por ejemplo, una ola de suicidios de viejitos. Y se suicidaban. Conseguían una o dos botellas de petróleo, de petróleo de carro. Tomaron uno o dos botellas y se murieron; una muerte terrible. Se tomaban una o dos botellas. Eso se dijo en una reunión donde yo estaba como periodista, pero a veces yo tenía un poco de ética de no utilizar eso en los libros que yo estaba escribiendo. Entonces yo tenía un poco de ética, ¿no? De separar las cosas y no aprovecharme, ¿no? de mi trabajo como periodista. Y así pasaron cosas terribles, realmente. La gente se quedó muy abandonada. No solo era que no había alimentos, sino que no había medicina, no había aspirina. Años sin conseguir una aspirina. Podíamos sobrevivir un poquito los que teníamos familia en Estados Unidos, en Miami. Y, bueno, ya te digo, es como outsiders, no. Cada quién buscando su pequeño, haciendo su pequeño mundo, y no tiene nada que ver con el estado, con la política. Porque esto no resuelve nada. Pues, yo tengo que resolver mi vida. Es así. Eso genera, por supuesto, mucha agresividad. Genera mucha violencia: violencia de palabras, violencia de pensamientos y violencia de acción.

M: ¿Crees que es posible formar una comunidad alternativa en vez de solamente haber individuos fuera del sistema, o tienes una visión totalmente individualista, más cínica, de esta situación?

PJG: Es una visión más individualista, más, quizás un poco cínica, y quizás hasta pesimista, ¿no? Al extremo de que la mayor parte de la gente que está así, en esos ambientes tan cerrados, la única solución que encuentra en su vida es irse del país. No es solo en Cuba. Si tú vas a España como estoy yendo yo desde el año 1998, te das cuenta de la enorme cantidad de inmigrantes que hay de Santo Domingo, de Ecuador. Bueno pasa lo mismo en Estados Unidos, en Canadá, en Francia, en Italia, en todos lados, ¿no? La gente lo que hace es irse. Así que no es solo un fenómeno de Cuba, y allí estamos hablando de un fenómeno mundial. Pasa igual en África. La gente no quiere morirse porque no hay medios. ¿Qué vamos a hacer, vivir con qué? ¿Qué vamos a hacer? ¿Para qué? No tiene sentido, ¿no? Y entonces, la gente lo que hace es irse. Los haitianos, Haití es un caso de esos, ¿no? La gente lo que quiere es irse. En España hay un grave problema con los africanos que atraviesan el estrecho de Gibraltar y tratan de entrar en España de manera subrepticia. A veces los cogen, a veces pueden entrar. Así que eso es lo que hay.

M: Cambiando de tema, muchos críticos dicen que tus obras son muy sexistas. ¿Cómo ves el rol del machismo en lo que has escrito?

PJG: Sí, mira. ¿Tú sabes qué pasa? La corrección política, hace mucho daño al arte, a la literatura actualmente. Ese tipo de académico que rechazan, que dicen, "¡Ay, es machista!," que es esto, que es lo otro, son personas muy limitadas. ¿Qué entonces tratan con la corrección política?: "¡Ay, respeto a los gay! ¡Ay, respeto a los negros! ¡Ay, respeto a las minorías étnicas!" Eso está muy bien. Yo estoy muy de acuerdo con eso, de que se respeten. Pero en arte y en literatura, el autor, el pintor, o lo que sea, necesita como una especie de licencia poética para poder llegar a lo profundo del ser humano. Si yo estoy escribiendo sobre gente de Centro Habana que son racistas y que son machistas, ¡son así! Esas personas son racistas y son machistas. Incluso no solo blancos contra negros. El negro es racista contra su propia raza, contra su propia gente y contra el blanco. Entonces trata al blanquito con desprecio. El negro por ejemplo dice de una negra que es conflictiva: "no, yo prefiero a una blanca así de ojos azules, rubia de ojos grises, blanquita. ¿Por qué? Porque la negra es muy conflictiva." Entonces cuando le preguntas a ese tipo de negra, no estoy hablando de mujeres con más educación, ella dice: "los negros son borrachos, y son mentirosos, y son vagos." Un negro es vago, mentiroso, y borracho. Yo les escribo así. Yo les escribo así sabiendo que me voy a buscar problemas con los académicos, con los editores. "Ay, ¿para qué esto? ¡Agrede a los negros!" Que es así en la realidad que yo vivo. ¡Es así! ¡Yo no estoy hablando de Obama! ¡Yo no estoy escribiendo sobre Obama! ¡Yo no estoy escribiendo sobre Martin Luther King! Yo estoy escribiendo de negros que son racistas y que son machistas. ¡Acéptalo de esa manera! Ahora porque tú no quieres, porque tú eres académico y entonces la corrección política. Mira, yo diría la mayoría de los escritores no quieren buscarse problemas en Estados Unidos, en España. Y el resultado es que estamos entrando en una etapa de literatura aburrida. Hemos entrado. ¡Estamos inmersos ya en una terrible etapa de literatura aburrida! Porque los escritores no se atreven a profundizar en cosas que les puedan traer problemas después, que le pueden traer este tipo de crítica. ¿Por qué a Bukowski casi no se le estudia en los medios académicos? ¿Por qué? Creo que Bukowski está bastante separado de los medios académicos. Hay muy poca gente que reconozca a Bukowski como un escritor. Me parece que fue un hombre que escribió con mucha fuerza y con mucha sinceridad. Por supuesto que fue un hombre culto que sabía de música. Sabía de literatura. Sabía de todo. Pero su posición estética era esconder todo ese conocimiento. Que es lo mismo que hago yo en mis libros. Yo he leído todo. Conozco toda la música. De todo. Pero no me da la gana en mis libros ponerme a hablar. A veces dejo caer algo así, por aquí, por allá, de Wagner de Beethoven, de esto y el otro, pero no es el énfasis que hago. Entonces, sucede eso. Aprovecho para decírtelo y es lamentable que suceda eso, que los escritores en aras de que sus libros sigan vendiendo, de que los editores no le pongan problemas, pues entonces se limitan, y no están haciendo una literatura con profundidad. En Estados Unidos quedan muy pocos escritores que se puedan leer con fuerza.

General Interest

"Ahora, por ejemplo:" "*ahora*" as a discursive deictic in Chilean Spanish

Mariška A. Bolyanatz
University of California, Los Angeles

1. INTRODUCTION

According to Silva-Corvalán ("Ahora" 67), the discourse marker *ahora* in Chilean Spanish has undergone (or is undergoing) a process of grammaticalization or subjectification. In other words, where *ahora* had existed previously as a sentential adverb, in Silva-Corvalán's work *ahora* has begun to resemble a conjunction (in her definition, "una forma no autónoma con posición fija" (*Sociolingüística* 219). *Ahora* can therefore be used as a discourse marker to signal a border between parts of a text or discourse (*Sociolingüística* 219). However, according to Silva-Corvalán ("Ahora" 80), it has yet to be proven that *ahora* is actually undergoing a change due to a lack of diachronic data. Silva-Corvalán's data consisted of a wide range of interviewees from the late 1990s, and to show that *ahora* has undergone a process of subjectification, I examine the uses of *ahora* from late 1970s Chilean Spanish.

In order to provide a comparable source of information to the data of Silva-Corvalán, I utilize a volume of *El habla culta de Santiago de Chile* (Rabanales and Contreras).[1] This volume contains transcripts of interviews carried out with current university students and university-educated older adults in Santiago, and is therefore similar to the conversation data collected by Silva-Corvalán. Following the categories delineated by Silva-Corvalán, I analyze one male and one female from the youngest and the oldest age groups cited in this study, for a total of 4 speakers. For each occurrence of *ahora* in the speech of these interviewees, I determine whether it is a temporal deictic (signifying "now," as opposed to in the past) or a discourse deictic (a connector which may serve to introduce a new topic). This determination is based on Silva-Corvalán's approach, which will be established in section 3. Following this analysis, I compare my findings to Silva-Corvalán's data, attempting to determine whether or not this can be considered a change in progress. Juola has shown through statistical analysis that language change can be measured, and can occur over centuries or in time periods as short as decades (77). Therefore, the lapse of twenty years between the data analyzed in this paper may represent a measurable linguistic change.

Though the discourse of only four speakers is analyzed here, Silva-Corvalán's hypothesis could be supported by the use of *ahora* as a discourse deictic simply by one speaker. Indeed, I find that the young male uses *ahora* in this way several times. Specifically, this speaker uses *ahora* to introduce speculative or argumentative discourse topics, to provide emphasis for a subsequent utterance, to convey his attitudes toward the content of his utterances and generally to guide his listener's inferences. These tokens provide diachronic data for the hypothesis put forth by Silva-Corvalán, and demonstrate that *ahora* had already begun to shift in meaning from a temporal to a discourse deictic during the late 1970s. Of course, further research should be done to confirm this preliminary assessment. However, using historical data in this way serves to provide initial evidence for this semantic shift.

2. Review of the Literature

Discourse markers, according to Portolés (25-26), can be defined as invariable linguistic units that do not exercise a syntactic function within the sentential predication, a definition in line with that of Schiffrin (237) who also adds that these markers can bracket units of talk. According to Schourup (230), this connective attribute is one of the three most important characteristics of discourse markers, as well as optionality and non-truth conditionality. By optionality, the author means syntactically optional: its absence does not alter the grammaticality of its host sentence. However, at the same time, a discourse marker cannot be seen as irrelevant or redundant, since, as Silva-Corvalán (*Sociolingüística* 214) and Portolés (26) state, these markers act as clues which guide the hearer in the inferences that he or she generates in a conversation. Typically, discourse markers are sentence—or utterance—initial, and can even appear in clusters of multiple markers. According to Schourup, this initial position relates to their 'superordinate' use to restrict the contextual interpretation of an utterance, again contributing to their 'guiding' function, restricting the hearer's possible inferences (233). The third characteristic of discourse markers, non-truth-conditionality, distinguishes these markers from 'content' words such as manner adverbial uses of words such as 'sadly,' which, unlike the uses of *ahora* in this paper, do not possess a deictic reading.

According to Schiffrin, *now* can be used as a temporal deictic in English in three distinct ways: it provides a temporal index in discourse time; it is ego-centered; and it may be evaluative (245).[2] As stated by Schourup, *now* and expressions like it (*you know, so, then,* etc.) "comprise a subset of those linguistic expressions thought not to affect the propositional content of utterances in which they occur" (227). *Now* is, in other words, a deictic: it may have a reference that is dependent on the immediate context of its utterance (cf. Horn 130), also known as indexicality (Cameron, "Aging" 210). Portolés provides a classification system of several different types of discourse markers, based on their potential pragmatic functions: information structures, connectors, reformulators, discursive operators, and contact control markers (135-146). As stated above, in this paper I will focus on the connector category, and more specifically, on the discourse marker *ahora* (*now*) in Chilean Spanish.

As a temporal deictic, *now* provides a temporal index for utterances within an emerging world of talk. In other words, *now* provides an index for the speaker's ideas, the orientation between speaker and hearer, and the footing established between them (Schiffrin 245). By ego-centered, Schiffrin means a space dominated by the producer of an utterance, and one that is focused on what the speaker him/herself is about to say. Additionally, Schiffrin proposes an evaluative element to *now*, claiming that speakers use *now* to introduce an evaluative statement within their utterance, highlighting "interpretive glosses for one's own talk which a speaker him/herself favors" (245).

However, Silva-Corvalán extends the definition of *ahora* in Spanish beyond that of a temporal deictic to that of a discourse deictic, claiming that it has undergone a process of subjectification. As cited in Torres Cacoullos and Schwenter, subjectification has been defined as a tendency for meanings to change from objective description of the external situation towards the expression of the speaker's *internal perspective or attitude* (348). Through this process, forms and constructions that initially express primarily *concrete*, *lexical* and *objective* meanings come to serve increasingly *abstract*, *pragmatic*, *interpersonal*, and *speaker-based* functions (348-9).

In her 1999 study, Silva-Corvalán analyzed approximately fifteen hours of recorded conversations with thirteen speakers from Santiago de Chile. These speakers ranged from 20-84 years old, and 6 were females and 7 males. Silva-Corvalán does not provide sociolinguistic correlates with her data, but does show that every speaker utilized *ahora* as a connector. Overall, she found that the temporal meaning of *ahora* was the most frequent in the data (604 of 770 tokens, 78.5%), followed by the pragmatic (or discourse) uses of *ahora* (148 of 770, 19.2%). The remaining tokens (18 of 770, 2%) she found to be indeterminate in terms of their interpretation.

As Silva-Corvalán states, this process of change (from propositional or textual meanings to expressive meanings) also connotes a conveyance of speakers' *attitudes* toward the content of their utterances ("Ahora" 68). She defines a temporal deictic use of *ahora* as one that includes the moment/immediate space of the utterance, has imprecise temporal limits, is opposed to *antes, entonces, luego* and *después*, and includes a sense of "opposition," which the author understands as opposition to the past (now vs. then/the past). We conceive of *ahora* as a contrastive discourse marker, as opposed to its use as a temporal adverb which modifies the sentential predicate ("Ahora" 70). A discourse deictic use of *ahora*, on the other hand, always appears in a sentence-initial position or is preceded by "*y*." Its contextual significance includes that of an introductory link between discourse content that is opposed to that of the previous utterance (*Sociolingüística* 225), or even as a connector between utterances "to meanings that are external to such utterance [*sic*]" ("Ahora" 70). As Tomioka states, this notion of opposition can appear in speech acts through the semantic notion of contrastiveness, often found in question-answer pairs, overtly contrasting statements ("not A but B"), correcting statements, clefts/ pseudo-clefts, and association with focus with adverbs like *only* and *always* (4). In other words, a temporal deictic situates an utterance in a particular space or time, whereas a discourse deictic connects (and even introduces) two utterances not necessarily related to each other, usually with some sort of evaluative element to its usage.

In this study, as the reader will note, each of the speakers employs a similar level of formality, thereby facilitating analysis. Labov has shown that the style in which a person speaks has an effect on their adherence to linguistic norms. As he indicates in his 1966 study, in casual speech, women tend to employ the more advanced linguistic forms, but "conform to the norm much more than do men of the same social group when using the most formal style" ("Social Stratification" 311-312). Trudgill's study, though it does not take style into account, shows that women employ forms that more closely approximate the standard or that are more prestigious than those employed by men (*Sociolingüística* 95). However, Fontanella de Weinberg, in a study regarding Bahía Blanca, found that younger women with a low-medium level of education tend to employ the newer variety more often (87). As we can see from these conflicting results, women use both the standard and the innovative forms of a variety. The relevance of each of these definitions and explorations will be demonstrated in the following sections, beginning with the methodology of this study.

3. METHODOLOGY

The materials for this investigation consist of four interviews within Volume One of *El habla culta de Santiago de Chile*, each of which was recorded in Santiago in 1979. All of the interviews analyzed in this investigation come from the "diálogos dirigidos" section, in which the interviewer converses with one or two participants, stimulating the conversation. This section will provide several demographic details of the four interviewees. Following this brief presentation, the uses of *ahora* in each of the interviews will be presented, as well as a concise categorization of each usage as either a temporal or a discursive deictic. As in every type of analysis of discourse, it is necessary to contextualize the utterance in order to ensure its correct evaluation (cf. Goodwin and Heritage).

Each of the four participants qualify as "cultos," or middle-class and higher in Chilean terms during the late 1970s. The first two participants belong to the youngest age group (25-35 years old). Participant one, Jimena, is a female, 27 years of age, a specialist in political and administrative sciences. Her interview took approximately 45 minutes. The second participant, Mauricio, is a 27-year-old chemist, whose interview took approximately 43 minutes. The second two participants belong to the oldest age group (56-75 years old). Participant three, Gladys, is a 62-year-old woman, whose interview took approximately 39 minutes. Gladys is a social worker and retired French teacher. Participant 4, Julio, is a 64-year-old doctor, whose interview took approximately 46 minutes.

Silva-Corvalán's study provides several guidelines for the analysis of *ahora* within the corpus of the *Habla culta de Santiago de Chile* volume ("Ahora" 73-74). The interviews are coded using the following guidelines:

(1) Temporal deictic:
   a. Basic meaning: "present perspective of the speaker"
   b. Contextual meaning: "present perspective of the speaker + opposition"

(2) Discourse deictic:
   Contextual meaning: "present perspective of the discourse + connector introducing discourse content slightly opposed to that of the preceding utterances"

In other words, a temporal deictic *ahora* is one that situates an utterance in a particular space and time, usually in opposition to an earlier mention of time. A discourse deictic use of *ahora* always appears in a sentence-initial position (or after *y*), and connects two utterances not necessarily related to each other temporally.

This paper will attempt to provide answers to the following research questions:

(1) a. Is *ahora* present in the 1979 data as a discursive deictic, or only as a temporal deictic?
   b. If *ahora* is present as a discursive deictic, how is it used specifically?
   c. If *ahora* is present as a discursive deictic, is there a distinction between the ages of the speakers who utilize *ahora* as a discursive deictic?
   d. Is there a difference in the way males and females use *ahora*?

The corresponding hypotheses are the following:

(2) a. Yes. *Ahora* as a discursive deictic will be present in the 1979 data.
   b. *Ahora* will be used in similar ways as it is in Silva-Corvalán's data, but perhaps in less broad ways. In other words, speakers will use *ahora* as a discursive deictic with a more limited range of functions than those used in the 1999 study.
   c. Yes. The younger speakers will use *ahora* as a discursive deictic more than the older speakers.
   d. Yes. As with many different types of language change, women tend to be the originators (such as Fontanella de Weinberg 90,

Sociolingüística 249). Therefore, such will be the case in this situation: women will use *ahora* as a discursive deictic more often than men.

It is important that the preliminary nature of this study is kept in mind. Only four speakers are studied, but as mentioned above, this initial assessment provides evidence for Silva-Corvalán's previously unattested hypothesis. The data of these speakers and their corresponding analyses will be presented in the next section.

4. DATA AND ANALYSIS

The first speaker, Jimena, utilized *ahora* a total of eleven times during her interview. The stated topics of her interview were "varios," but consist of a discussion of her job in Prison Services, her workplace environment, and women in the workplace. In (3), the interviewer asks Jimena about her current work situation, and Jimena responds, telling the interviewer about the freedom allotted in her office versus other departments at her place of work. The use of *ahora* as a temporal deictic is exemplified. In lines 5-6 Jimena discusses what will happen in the future: specifically that there will not be as many problems at her place of work because there will be more staff. This temporal contrast between "now" and "the future" is represented through the use of the subjunctive mood (*una vez que se cree*). In this way, we can see that Jimena uses *ahora* in this utterance as a temporal discourse marker.

(3) 1   Somos responsables de cumplir la labor que él me encarga a mí, pero si él la

2   aprueba, es cosa de él. Entonces, no es como los otros departamentos, que

3   tienen que cumplir tal labor porque está estipulada y deben cumplir

4   forzosamente. Nosotros no; somos más libres. Y una vez que se cree la

5   oficina, ya no va a haber tanto problema, porque vamos a ser más personas.

6   Ahora soy yo sola, y una persona sola no puede hacer todo, es una cosa tan

7   amplia.

In (4) and (5), the interviewer asks Jimena about her school situation, specifically the examination experience. Also, (4) and (5) are representations of *ahora* as a temporal deictic. In both of these examples, the speaker uses *ahora* to contrast with a verb in the past tense (*estaba* and *tuve* respectively), switching her reference from the past to the present.

(4) 1   Es bien bonita la carrera. Nosotros nos podemos especializar—bueno, hasta

    2   cuando estaba yo, porque ahora está con un plan nuevo, renovado, la escuela,

    3   así que ya no es lo mismo que cuando yo estudiaba.

(5) 1   Mira, la verdad es que definiciones hay varias y yo las supe todas cuando tuve

    2   que dar mi examen de Personal, pero ahora yo no me acuerdo de ninguna

    3   que te la pudiera recitar así, es decir . . .

(6) is similar to (4) and (5), with a morphological switch of temporality (*era, estaba* to present tense *se desempeña*). In addition, the temporal adverb *antes* is used in line 1, which also contrasts with the present 'now.' In this way, *ahora* is exemplified as a temporal deictic.

(6) 1   Bueno, yo lo encuentro magnífico, porque la mujer antes era tan tontona,

    2   pues, oye, que toda la vida estaba, o en las labores de casa o en un trabajo

    3   totalmente sencillo; pero ahora la mujer se desempeña a la par que el

    4   hombre, pues.

(7) through (10) each proceed from the same section of the interview, in which Jimena and the interviewer discuss the role of women in the workplace and specifically among her female colleagues and peers. The use of *ahora* in (7) and (8) could be replaced by another temporal adverb such as "currently," which exemplifies Jimena's use of *ahora* as contrasted with the past. (9) and (10) also represent the use of *ahora* as a temporal discourse marker, contrasting a past time period (represented by the verbal past-tense morphology) with the present situation in which her female colleagues find themselves (specifically, with children). In addition, (10) includes a citation within a citation, in which Jimena quotes a third speaker (the non-specific *tú,*) in order to insert a commentary about the particular situation (cf. Labov "Transformation" 383-385).

(7) 1   No sé, ahora, en estos últimos meses, pero hasta hace poco tiempo sucedía, y

    2   ¿sabes dónde? más que nada, en ENDESA.

(8) 1   En ENDESA . . . eh . . . el profesional, para ellos, era hombre. Pero ahora último,

    2   hará cosa de unos seis meses atrás, han entrado bastantes compañeras de

    3   nosotros . . .

(9) 1   Yo tengo compañeras, se casaron e . . . en mitad de la carrera y terminaron por

    2   el hecho de terminarla, pero ahora están con sus guaguas y no han trabajado

    3   más.

(10) 1   Y luego se aclimata, y después, si tú dejas pasar el tiempo y te dedicas

      2   después que tienes tus niños grandes y dices: "ahora me voy a buscar un

      3   trabajo," ¿dónde vas a trabajar si la experiencia la has perdido, no tienes

      4   nada?

Though (11) does not provide a contrast to an earlier utterance, since it appears in between an overt subject and its verb rather than in sentence-initial position, we can categorize it as a temporal adverb which modifies the verb 'live' (*vivo*). Similarly, the use of *ahora* in (12) coincides with the specific 'in May,' illustrating a temporal use of the marker.

(11) 1   Claro, mientras tanto uno no tiene ni un problema. Uno . . . yo ahora vivo con

      2   mis papás, tengo todo, no me falta; es de esperar que casada tampoco.

(12) 1   . . . estuvo bailando casi toda la noche conmigo; después hicimos una cuantas

      2   salidas en grupo juntos, y él siempre conmigo, y hasta que al final salimos

      3   pololeando. Ya vamos . . . llevamos dos años ya casi. Ahora los enteramos en

      4   mayo.

In sum, each of Jimena's uses of *ahora* represents a temporal deictic, contrasting a past or future referent with one in the present. Zero uses of *ahora* as discourse deictics appear in this particular interview.

The second speaker, Mauricio, the young male participant, utilizes *ahora* a total of eight times, both as a temporal and a discursive deictic. The subject of this guided interview is "actividades profesionales del informante." Each of these first three uses of *ahora* by Mauricio exemplifies a discursive deictic use. The uses of *ahora* in ((13), line 4) and ((14), line 2) both serve to mark information that adds to a prior collection of items (cf. Schiffrin 237). As Silva-Corvalán stipulates, each of the uses of *ahora* appear in sentence-initial position, and function as an "introductory link" between sets of discourse that are unrelated—or even opposed to one another—(*Sociolingüística* 225). The use of *ahora* in (15), line 3 on the other hand, branches into a subtopic that had been previously introduced, and Mauricio uses *ahora* here to guide his hearer to a change in subject.

(13) 1   Aquí en Chile tenemos una vegetación muy rica en flores principalmente,

      2   plantas que son totalmente desconocidas desde el punto de vista químico, ya

      3   que los . . . eh . . . por ejemplo, ¿cómo explicarte? . . . eh . . . los olores que tienen

      4   . . . se . . . provienen de ciertos componentes químicos bien específicos. Ahora . . .

      5   eh . . . por ejemplo, el . . . eh . . . boldo, el agua de boldo, que aquí es tan

      6   conocida, tiene ciertos componentes químicos . . .

(14) 1 . . . Tiene ciertos componentes químicos . . . que actúan farmacológicamente
2 sobre ciertos . . . eh . . . malestares del organismo. Ahora, la . . . el aislamiento de
3 estos compuestos, ya sea . . . eh . . . de tipo colorantes, de tipo aromático . . .
4 puede conducir a que Chile se convierta potencialmente en un exportador de estos
5 principios activos . . .

(15) 1 La gente no . . . no mira hacia los lados. Está o demasiado preocupada de sus
2 problemas personales o demasiado preocupada de su trabajo, pero no se
3 preocupa por el resto del mundo. Ahora . . . eh . . . me gustaría si tú me puedes
4 explicar más qué concepto te interesa que . . . que desarrolle, porque esto es . . .

Though he does not categorize *now* as a contrastive marker, Fraser defines these markers as signaling that the following utterance is in some way a denial or a contrast of some proposition associated with the preceding discourse, which I claim is an element of Mauricio's discourse uses of *ahora* (987).

In (16), we see a morphological contrast: in lines 1-3, Mauricio is discussing the situation at the university from the past year. In line 4, *ahora* can be seen as a temporal deictic due to the switch in tense (from past to present). However, *ahora* in sentence-initial position in this utterance also serves to introduce a new topic: academic publications. As stated above, Mauricio contrasts lines 4-6 with 1-3, introducing a new but related topic, and for this reason, I categorize this particular use as a discourse deictic.

(16) 1 El año pasado, de la Facultad, casi el diez por ciento, me atrevería a decir, de
2 los profesionales que aquí trabajan normalmente, es decir, docentes, se
3 encontraban en el extranjero haciendo estudios de perfeccionamiento.
4 Ahora . . . eh . . . en cuanto a publicaciones, eh . . . porque ésa es otra . . . otro de
5 los factores que se . . . los cuales se cataloga a un . . . a un equipo, a un
6 establecimiento de trabajo, en la Universidad.

In contrast, the use of *ahora* in (17) exemplifies a temporal deictic. Mauricio utilizes this marker to differentiate the past (in which many of his colleagues did not make it through his major program), from the present (in which the recent reforms to the education system may allow for more opportunities for students).

(17) 1 Del total, de esos veinticinco, creo que se irán a recibir unos ocho o nueve. El
2 resto, o desertó porque no le gustó, o no se . . . o no fue capaz, sencillamente,
3 porque, como te decía anteriormente, el de . . . el sistema de . . . de estudios es

4   demasiado intensivo. Ahora con . . . con la reforma se pretende cambiar un

5   poco el sistema y darle al alumno más posibilidades . . .

In (18) we see *ahora* used as a discourse deictic yet again. Mauricio utilizes *ahora* as a transition to a new (but related) thought; he does not change from past to present tense or make other references to time.

(18) 1   ... este tema es porque conocía al . . . a la persona que en este momento

2   trabajaba con esa línea de . . . de ideas y me agradó la forma en que esta

3   persona podía dirigir a la gente. Ahora, me dirigí . . . eh . . . me . . . me entusiasmé

4   por este trabajo porque podría realizarlo . . .

Mauricio begins (19) by discussing his current job situation, in which he is involved in a project that he does not particularly like. However, in line 2, he reverts back to the preterit imperfect (e.g. *decía*), and then uses *ahora* to temporally contrast his utterances.

(19) 1   En este momento he trabajado aquí. Pretendo en lo posible darle un corte

2   final a esto, sacar una publicación y cambiar de tema. Como te decía, me

3   gustaría cambiar ahora hacia algo . . . a . . . de tipo aplicado. Esto de los

4   microorganismos también es aplicado . . .

(20) is another use of *ahora* as a discourse deictic. Mauricio begins this utterance by discussing employment, and uses the present tense (lines 1-3). In line 3, Mauricio uses *ahora* as a transition between independent utterances, introducing the topic that he will address from lines 3-5, 'brain drain' in Chile. In addition, due to the verb clause 'returning to the professional that escapes/ leaves Chile' (*volviendo al profesional que se fuga de Chile*) in lines 3-4, we can see that he is returning to a previously introduced topic. We do not see any morphological or lexical use that would suggest a contrast of time.

(20) 1   Existen miles de otros trabajos, tantos y cuanto más productivos y más

2   beneficiosos para nosotros, y que, en ningún grado . . . eh . . . de ninguna

3   manera, lo denigran. Ahora, en . . . en cuanto al universitario, volviendo al

4   profesional que se fuga de Chile, yo personalmente también soy partidario de

5   que si no puedo desarrollarme como químico aquí . . .

As the reader will note, Mauricio uses *ahora* as a discursive deictic several times. Each of these uses is analyzed further in the next section, in order to provide stronger evidence for the hypothesis of Silva-Corvalán.

The discussion of the third participant introduces a second age group. At 62 years of age, Gladys falls into the upper age category put forth by Silva-Corvalán. Her interview was conducted regarding the topics of pedagogical experiences and travel. The participant, a French teacher, recalls her experience as a student of Latin, and throughout her interview uses *ahora* only to express a temporal contrast. In (21), Gladys uses past-tense verb morphology and the phrase 'in that time' (*en ese tiempo*) to signify that she is talking about events situated in the past; specifically, how her Latin teacher treated her and her classmates. In line 3, Gladys uses *ahora* to contrast previous, past-situated utterances with present-situated ones. Since she is retired, she does not know how Latin classes function in the current school system, but supposes that they occur in a certain way. In line 4, Gladys uses *ahora* a second time within the same utterance, and once again contrasts the previous utterances of lines 1-3 with what she will say next: that she assumes that currently (when this interview took place) pedagogy is more intimate, more like a dialogue between a teacher and a student.

(21) 1   Así que no . . . no porque me tocó a mí en la clase pasada ya . . . ya voy a dejar

2   pasar a la otra semana mi turno; no; teníamos que estar . . . porque nos pillaba.

3   Nos interrogaba; era bien guapo, bien estricto. Ahora no sé cómo serán las

4   clases; creo que ahora más es conversación así como íntima, un diálogo entre

5   maestro y alumno; allá no; en ese tiempo siempre estaba la categoría del

6   maestro en su tarima enseñando, y los alumnos tomando apuntes o . . . o

7   estudiando, aprendiendo de otra manera.

In the next excerpt, the interviewer asks Gladys if she misses teaching/pedagogy. Though she does not explicitly contrast the proposition of *ahora* with anything in the past (i.e. lines 2-4) the hearer can infer that when she taught years ago, in her view, the situation was dissimilar. Since this utterance refers to the same subject of dialogue as (21)—teaching and pedagogy when Gladys was a teacher contrasted with the present-day—we can attribute a temporally contrastive meaning to her use of *ahora*.

(22) 1   No; no echo nada de menos. Cuando veo estas cosas que están pasando

2   ¡menos! Fíjese que me han dicho que ahora las alumnas tienen miedo de ir . . .

3   de esas niñas seguramente tímidas y que no comparten con los muchachos

4   su . . . sus actitudes así, prepotentes, nada de eso.

In addition, (23) belongs to the same speech run (i.e. not inter-rupted by the interviewer) as (22), in which Gladys continues discussing the differences between when she was a teacher and the current situation of language learning. Again, in this last use of *ahora* by Gladys within her interview, we read a sense of opposition between how things were in the past, as compared to how they are (or must be) now (in the present). Lines 1-7 consist almost entirely of preterit imperfect verb conjugations, signifying a past-situated narrative. In line 8, Gladys supposes through the use of the temporally motivated discourse marker that things must be different now than in her day.

(23) 1   . . . les habían dicho más bien que les iban a dar facilidades para levantar su
2   población, entonces ellos se habían tomado la escuela, y las alumnas tenían
3   que presentar toda suerte de credenciales para poder entrar a clases, y dice
4   que era . . . las caras medios patibularias de los individuos, bien entonados y
5   bien puestos en su línea, que no aceptaban cualquier cosa, y las echaban; a
6   muchas no las querían aceptar porque no traían to [sic] . . . los permisos
7   condicionados, permisos tales y cuales que ellos tenían que revisar. Yo creo
8   que debe [sic] ser bien difícil ahora las cosas.

In sum, Gladys uses ahora only as a temporal deictic, not a dis-course deictic, similar to the fourth and final interview in this series with a male from the oldest age group. Julio, a 64-year-old doctor in Santiago, was questioned on the topic of *cuestiones médicas*. Within six lines of discourse, we see a temporal opposition: in line 2, the speaker states that he cannot remember the name of something "in this moment," but then interrupts himself in line 5 to say that 'now' he remembers. This reasoning leads the author to categorize this use of *ahora* as a temporal deictic.

(24) 1   Posteriormente, aparecieron otras reacciones, como la reacción de un sapo,
2   un sapo cuyo nombre no me recuerdo en este momento (las características
3   del sapo) y que se llama la "reacción de Galli Mainini" . . . eh . . . argentino. La
4   otra . . . un . . . era autor alemán, médico alemán, y antes de eso . . . antes de eso
5   . . . antes de la reacción de Friedman ya se practicaba—ahora me acuerdo—se
6   practicaba la "reacción de Aschheim-Zondel."

The second and final use of *ahora* by this speaker is found toward the middle of the interview, while the interviewer and the participant are discussing immunizations:

(25) 1   Los virus se cultivan en huevo, en fin; tienen dificultades, y estas técnicas no

2   están en mi . . . en mi conocimiento del problema. Eso tal vez lo prepara el

3   Bacterólogo [sic], ¿ah? Pero generalmente el período viral . . . y ahora vienen

4   todas estas vacunas que se dan en gotas también ¿no? pa' los niños.

This use of *ahora* is correlated with an utterance several lines before, due to the fact that the subject matter of both (25) and (26) is immunizations. Neither of these utterances is in opposition to previous statements, or prior uses of the past tense. However, the listener/reader is also able to infer that vaccinations did not always exist in droplet form, but do in the present (the immediate space of the utterance), categorizing this as a temporal use of the phrase.

(26) 1   Pa' mí, yo considero que hoy día la vacuna oral es superior a cualquiera de

2   los . . . de los métodos de antibióticos que existen.

Table 1 represents graphically each of the uses of *ahora* by each of the participants.

TABLE I. Uses of *ahora* by each participant

Participant	Uses of *ahora* as a temporal deictic	Uses of *ahora* as a discourse deictic	Total *n*:
Jimena	11	0	**11**
Mauricio	2	**6**	**8**
Gladys	4	0	**4**
Julio	2	0	**2**

As the reader will note, the youngest speaker (Jimena) utilized *ahora* at the greatest rate (11 uses in approximately 40 minutes of conversation). Her male counterpart in the younger age group, Mauricio, utilized *ahora* at the second greatest rate (8 uses in approximately the same amount of time). The older speakers Gladys and Julio used *ahora* less often, four and two times, respectively. Of a total of 25 uses of *ahora*, 19 of them (76%) were used as temporal deictics, while the remaining 6 uses of ahora (24%) represent discourse deictics.

Interestingly, these ratios are approximately similar to those of Silva-Corvalán's study conducted 20 years later (19.2% of the uses of *ahora* manifested in her work were discourse deictic). Nonetheless, as opposed to Silva-Corvalán's study, the only participant that utilized *ahora* as a discourse deictic was Mauricio, the male from the younger demographic. Silva-Corvalán does not define which speakers used which types of deictics in her study, but she does specify that "*ahora* as a connector [was] attested in the speech of *all* the speakers studied"

("Ahora" 70; she uses "connector" as another term for discourse deictic). Therefore, we can see that the use of *ahora* as a discourse marker (and not simply a sentential, temporal adverb) may have been extended in the twenty years between the studies.

5. DISCUSSION AND CONCLUSIONS

Below are the research questions as presented in (1), restated as (27):

(27) a. Is *ahora* present in the 1979 data as a discursive deictic, or only as a temporal deictic?

b. If *ahora* is present as a discursive deictic, how is it used specifically?

c. Again, if *ahora* is present as a discursive deictic, is there a distinction between the ages of the speakers who utilize *ahora* as a discursive deictic?

d. Is there a difference in the way males and females use *ahora*?

First, we find that *ahora* as a discursive deictic is indeed present in the 1979 data, confirming Hypothesis 1. Second, we find that *ahora* as a discursive deictic is used to contrast a previous utterance, to call attention or emphasize, to mark information that adds to a prior collection of items, and overall to guide the hearer's inferences. The specific uses of *ahora* as a discursive deictic as used by Mauricio will be discussed further in this section. Regarding research question three, we find our hypothesis to be supported: the only speaker who used *ahora* as a discourse deictic belonged to the younger age group. However, in this same vein, hypothesis four was not supported: instead of the younger female using *ahora* as a discourse deictic as anticipated, the only speaker who used it was the younger male, Mauricio.

However, the finding that the participants did in fact use *ahora* as a discourse deictic in the late 1970s supports Silva-Corvalán's work only in part. In order to support Silva-Corvalán's theory that *ahora* has undergone a process of grammaticalization, the next step is to examine each of Mauricio's uses of *ahora* as a discourse deictic. According to Silva-Corvalán, the use of *ahora* as a connector is "strongly motivated, or at least favored, by speculative or argumentative discourse topics, and that when used as a connector it is not necessarily separated by a pause (or prosodic break) from the following utterance" ("Ahora" 70).[3] In addition, as previously stated, *ahora* may also have an emphatic function; that is, emphasizing or calling attention to the content of the discourse (Lamíquiz 12). Let us examine Mauricio's six uses of *ahora* as a discourse deictic for each of these features.

In (28), Mauricio speaks about the vegetation in Chile, and after the use of the discourse marker, seems to speak to something about which he is an expert: chemistry. It is possible that this use of *ahora* has an emphatic function (Lamíquiz 13), but the author prefers not to speculate further about this particular example.

(28) 1   Aquí en Chile tenemos una vegetación muy rica en flores principalmente,

2   plantas que son totalmente desconocidas desde el punto de vista químico, ya

3   que los . . . eh . . . por ejemplo, ¿cómo explicarte? . . . eh . . . los olores que

4   tienen . . . se... provienen de ciertos componentes químicos bien específicos.

5   Ahora . . . eh . . . por ejemplo, el . . . eh . . . boldo, el agua de boldo, que aquí es

6   tan conocida, tiene ciertos componentes químicos . . .

In (29), we see a use of *ahora* potentially motivated by the introduction of a topic about which the speaker is speculating or hypothesizing (cf. Silva-Corvalán "Ahora" 70).

(29) 1   . . . Tiene ciertos componentes químicos... que actúan farmacológicamente

2   sobre ciertos . . . eh . . . malestares del organismo. Ahora, la . . . el aislamiento de

3   estos compuestos, ya sea . . . eh . . . de tipo colorantes, de tipo aromático . . .

4   puede conducir a que Chile se convierta potencialmente en un exportador de estos

5   principios activos. . . .

(30) is one of the only occasions on which we see the speaker approach an argumentative style; he seems to be reaching a point of irritation with the vagueness of the interviewer. Here, we see an obvious change in attitude introduced by *ahora*.

(30) 1   La gente no . . . no mira hacia los lados. Está o demasiado preocupada de sus

2   problemas personales o demasiado preocupada de su trabajo, pero no se

3   preocupa por el resto del mundo. Ahora . . . eh . . . me gustaría si tú me puedes

4   explicar más qué concepto te interesa que . . . que desarrolle, porque esto es . . .

(31) is another example in which it seems as though the speaker wishes to call attention to his utterance, or the actual shift in topic.

(31) 1   El año pasado, de la Facultad, casi el diez por ciento, me atrevería a decir, de 2

los profesionales que aquí trabajan normalmente, es decir, docentes, se

3   encontraban en el extranjero haciendo estudios de perfeccionamiento.

4   Ahora . . . eh . . . en cuanto a <u>publicaciones,</u> eh . . . porque ésa es otra . . . otro de

5   los factores que se . . . los cuales se cataloga a un . . . a un equipo, a un

6   establecimiento de trabajo, en la Universidad.

The last two uses of *ahora* introduce utterances that convey a particular attitude of the speaker. In (32), Mauricio uses *ahora* to introduce his opinion and emotion regarding a particular subject: a job that he realized he was capable of doing. In (33), *ahora* reintroduces a topic that he had already discussed with his interlocutor, and then Mauricio continues to express a particular opinion on the subject, sharing his attitudes with the interviewer. As the reader will note, each of Mauricio's six uses of *ahora* comes after a prosodic pause (communicated orthographically through a period).

(32) 1   . . . este tema es porque conocía al . . . a la persona que en este momento

2   trabajaba con esa línea de . . . de ideas y me agradó la forma en que esta

3   persona podía dirigir a la gente. Ahora, me dirigí . . . eh . . . me . . . <u>me entusiasmé</u>

4   <u>por este trabajo porque podría realizarlo</u> . . .

(33) 1   Existen miles de otros trabajos, tantos y cuanto más productivos y más

2   beneficiosos para nosotros, y que, en ningún grado . . . eh . . . de ninguna

3   manera, lo denigran. Ahora, en . . . en cuanto al universitario, volviendo al

4   profesional que se fuga de Chile, <u>yo personalmente también soy partidario de</u>

5   <u>que si no puedo desarrollarme como químico aquí</u> . . .

Now that we have discussed Mauricio's uses of *ahora* as a discursive deictic, it is also necessary to thoroughly examine the results of Silva-Corvalán's study, which are presented in 1999, twenty years later. The results of Silva-Corvalán's study include frequent uses of *ahora* in what she calls "modal" speech acts, or qualification, condition and hypothesis ("Ahora" 79). It is due to these uses, she states, that most strongly support the hypothesis that this form is undergoing a change. In her data, there were frequent associations between *ahora* and a type of discourse that "invites the expression of the speaker's subjective attitudes, thus leading to the association of *ahora* with modality, a process that may be appropriately described as 'subjectifying' grammaticalization" ("Ahora" 79).

In addition, according to Silva-Corvalán, the development of a new modality for *ahora* does not mean that its old modality as a temporal deictic will be lost. Rather, as Heine et al. states (20), "semantic layering" may occur: "older meanings are not discarded but remain and coexist with the new meanings; different discourse contexts are compatible with one or another meaning of the form, and in turn promote the development of innovative interpretations" ("Ahora" 79).

Several issues with the present study must be taken into account. First, as shown, *ahora* appeared more in the discourse of one of the younger speakers than of the older speakers, though neither group utilized the marker to a great extent. Since it was a guided interview in a formal style, it is possible that the participants did not have the opportunity to approach a more narrative style (cf. Labov, "Social Stratification" 308-311) or provide evaluation of their utterances. It is also possible that the younger speakers simply happened to present contexts of language use in which *ahora* was useful or required.

In summary, through the excerpts of interviews transcribed in 1979 in Santiago, we see that *ahora* had already begun to undergo the process of subjectification in late 1979, shifting its meaning from that of a temporal deictic to a discursive deictic. Evidently, it is possible that this change had begun earlier. However, further research that utilizes even earlier sources will need to be undertaken in order to confirm this possibility. Specifically, Mauricio's six uses of *ahora* as a discursive deictic exemplify this shift. His uses of *ahora*, as stated by the literature, are motivated by speculative or argumentative discourse topics, may function to provide emphasis for the subsequent utterance, convey his attitudes toward the content of his utterances and overall, guide his listener's inferences.

That these uses of the innovative meaning of *ahora* are found in the younger age group aligns with the literature on language change (Cameron "Aging" 210, Rissel 279, Fontanella de Weinberg 57, Moreno de Alba 369, Labov 311-312, Lavandera 10). The fact that there is a difference in the uses of *ahora* across the age groups between these diachronic studies may suggest that there is a change in progress. However, as with any study on language shift, these results must be evaluated with a critical eye. As Rissel shows, the effect of gender is not necessarily uniform across a community (279-282). Additionally, Cameron ("Language" 288) and Silva-Corvalán (*Sociolingüística* 101-103) highlight the issues of age-gradation, in which throughout life, people grow, mature and pass through various stages of life. The apparent language change presented in these two studies could perhaps be simply a function of individual linguistic change.

In addition, Cameron ("Language" 290) cautions against diagnosing language change based on only one social or stylistic pattern. It would be necessary to examine several variables at once, in order to make this determination. This preliminary study is based on four speakers, all from the same socioeconomic stratum, speaking in a similarly formal style. In order to provide more conclusive evidence of a change in progress, the speech of many more participants would have to be evaluated. These analyses would need to take into account age, gender, socioeconomic status, style and, of course, context of speech.

Notes

1. This volume is part of a project that collects and transcribes the speech of upper class, educated speakers from the capital cities in the Iberian Peninsula and Latin America. This project was spearheaded by the late Juan M. Lope Blanch of the Universidad Autónoma Nacional de México.

2. The uses and analyses of now/*ahora* may or may not be the same in both English and Spanish. However, such a discussion is outside of the scope of the present paper.

3. The reader may notice that several uses of *ahora* in Mauricio's speech are followed by pauses (for example, in (28) and (30)). However, due to the presence and ubiquity of the pauses in the rest of his discourse, I have chosen not to take these pauses into account when determining the functions of his uses of *ahora*.

Works Cited

Cameron, Richard. "Language change or changing selves: Direct quotation strategies in the Spanish of San Juan, Puerto Rico." *Diachronica* 17 (2000): 249-292. Print.

———. "Aging, age, and sociolinguistics." *The Handbook of Hispanic Sociolinguistics*. Ed. Manuel Díaz-Campos. Malden, MA: Wiley-Blackwell, 2011. 207-229. Print.

Fontanella de Weinberg, Maria Beatriz. "Comportamiento ante -*s* de hablantes femeninos y masculinos del español bonaerense." *Romance Philology* 27 (1973): 50-58. Print.

Fraser, Bruce. "What are discourse markers?" *Journal of Pragmatics* 31 (1996): 931-952. Print.

Goodwin, Charles and John Heritage. "Conversation Analysis." *Annual Review of Anthropology* 19 (1990): 283-307. Print.

Heine, Bernd, Ulrike Claudi and Friederike Hunnemyer. *Grammaticalization: A Conceptual Framework*. Chicago: University of Chicago Press, 1990. Print.

Horn, Laurence. "Pragmatic Theory." *Linguistic Theory: Foundations*. Ed. F. Newmeyer. Cambridge: Cambridge University Press, 1988. 113-145. Print.

Juola, Patrick. "The Time Course of Language Change." *Computers and the Humanities, Digital Media and Humanities Research: Selected Proceedings of ACH-ALLC* 37.1 (2003): 77-96. Print.

Labov, William. *The social stratification of English in New York City*. Washington, D.C.: Center for Applied Linguistics, 1966. Print.

———. "The transformation of experience in narrative syntax." *Language in the inner city: Studies in the Black English Vernacular*. Philadelphia: University of Pennsylvania Press, 1972. 354-396. Print.

Lamíquiz, Vidal. "Conexión conmutadora entre enunciados." *Sociolingüística Andaluza: Estudios sobre el Enunciado Oral* 8 (1993): 11-33. Print.

Lavandera, Beatriz. *Variación y signficado*. Buenos Aires: Librería Hachette, 1984. Print.

Moreno de Alba, José G. "Frecuencias de la asibilación de *Ixl* y /rr/ en Mexico." *Nueva Revista de Filología Hispánica* 21 (1972): 363-370. Print.

Portolés, José. *Marcadores del discurso*. Barcelona: Ariel, 1998. Print.

Rabanales, Ambrosio and Lidia Contreras, eds. *El habla culta de Santiago de Chile*. Tomo 1. Santiago: Universidad de Chile, Departamento de Linguística y Filología, Editorial Universitaria, 1979. Print.

Schiffrin, Deborah. *Discourse Markers*. Melbourne: Cambridge University Press, 1987. Print.

Schourup, Lawrence. "Discourse markers." *Lingua* 107 (1999): 227-65. Print.

Silva-Corvalán, Carmen. "Ahora: From temporal to discourse deixis." *Essays in Hispanic linguistics dedicated to Paul M. Lloyd*. Eds. R. J. Blake, D. L. Ranson and R. Wright. Newark, DE: Juan de la Cuesta, 1999. 67-81. Print.

———. *Sociolingüística y pragmática del español*. Washington, D.C.: Georgetown University Press, 2001. Print.

Torres Cacoullos, Rena, and Scott A. Schwenter. "Towards an operational notion of subjectification." *Berkeley Linguistics Society* 31 (2005): 347-358. Print.

Trudgill, Peter. *Sociolinguistics: An Introduction*. Harmondsworth: Penguin, 1974. Print.

Tomioka, Satoshi. "Contrastive Topics Operate on Speech Acts." *Information Structure from Different Perspectives*. Eds. Féry, C. and M. Zimmermann. Cambridge: Oxford University Press, 2009. 115-138. Print.

Accounting for Variation of Diminutive Formation in Porteño Spanish

Ingrid Norrmann-Vigil
University of California, Los Angeles

1. Introduction

Diminutive formation is a highly productive derivational process in Spanish, and it is commonly used to express the little and/or endearing form of the word being derived (Colina, 2003; Harris, 1969; Jaeggli, 1980). Diminutives can be derived from nouns, adjectives, and adverbs, as shown in example (1).[1]

(1)	nouns	['pes]	'fish'	→	[pese'sito]	'little fish'
	adjectives	[ara'ɣan]	'lazy'	→	[araɣan'sito]	'lazy (endearing form)'
	adverbs	[tem'prano]	'early'	→	[tempra'nito]	'early (endearing form)'

As shown in the previous example, the Spanish speaker has different allomorphs available for this process: *-it*, *-sit*, *-esit*.[2] This paper analyzes the puzzle that arises when the speaker decides which allomorph to use, taking into consideration that sometimes the speaker himself is ambivalent as to which one to affix, as in example (2):

(2) ['brokoli] 'broccoli' [broko'lito] vs. [brokoli'sito]

To account for this ambivalence, this paper uses a Maximum Entropy Model (Hayes and Wilson, 2008), a probabilistic theory that captures this free variation.

In addition to the choice of allomorphy shown in (1), for words ending in vowels, the speaker has the option of deleting or not deleting this vowel, shown in (3):

(3) ['kasa] 'house' [ka'sita]
     ['berðe] 'green' [berðe'sito]

This expands even more the possible number of outputs per input and the free variation found amongst speakers. Thus, although participants in this study agreed in the formation of diminutives for words ending in /é/ by 94% (X'e → Xe+'sit; e.g. [ka'fe] 'coffee' → [kafe'sito]), most generalizations are imperfect. Such is the case of words with three or more syllables ending in /i/, where 55% retained the final vowel and affixed -*sit* (e.g. ['taksi] 'taxi cab'→ [taksi'sito]) and 44% deleted the final vowel and affixed -*it* (e.g. ['taksi] → [ta'ksito]).[3]

1.1 Spanish Word Structure

1.1.1 Terminal Elements and Base Elements

Final segments of non-inflected words in Spanish can be divided into *terminal elements* (hereafter, TEs) and *base elements*. Harris (1994) states that terminal elements are suffixes with "no 'meaning' or 'function' in the ordinary sense; they serve only as overt phonological identifiers of several lexically arbitrary form classes into which all Spanish nouns, adjectives and adverb stems and derivational affixes are partitioned" (185). The norm in Spanish is for this TE to match in gender with the word (i.e., words ending in /a/ are normally feminine and words ending in /o/ are normally masculine). To this, Colina (2003) adds that TEs cannot be stressed; therefore according to her definition the final /á/ in [mam'a] 'mom' is not a terminal element (thus a base element), whereas final /a/ in ['kama] 'bed' is a terminal element because it is unstressed.

Regarding final /e/, different scholars have made different proposals; however, Colina (2003) claims it is also a TE. This is a controversial statement as the data is not entirely clear. Based on other derivational processes, final /e/ can either follow the pattern of TEs (i.e., deleting before affixation) or not (i.e., not deleting before affixation) as shown in example (4).

(4) [a'lambɾe]   'wire'   →   [alambɾ'aðo]   'wire fence'

　　 ['kaβle]   'cable'   →   [kaβle'aðo]   'group of cables'

However, this deletion process could also be attributed to a phonological process that occurs in specific environments, but a deeper analysis of this issue is beyond the scope of this work. In addition, following the class analysis proposed by Harris (1992), this paper assumes classes I and II (i.e., words with final /a/ and /o/) to be the only TEs in Spanish, leaving final /e/ as a base element. According to the data, /e/ follows the same patterns as final /u/ and /i/ with regard to diminutive formation. By considering final /e/ to be part of the base, the inclusion of unmotivated constraints can be avoided, thereby yielding a simpler grammar. Thus, this paper considers final stressless /a/ or /o/ (as in example 5) to be the only two TEs in Spanish.

(5) /a/   ['kam-a]   'bed'
     /o/   ['liβr-o]   'book'

Therefore, *base elements* include all consonants and the remaining vowels. The examples below illustrate final stressed /á/ and /ó/ (example 6), all final /i/ and /u/ (example 7), and all final /e/ as base elements (example 8).

(6) /á/   [ʧiri'pa]   'cloth diaper'
     /ó/   [boŋ'go]   'bongo'

(7) /i/   ['bondi]   'bus'
     /í/   [ma'ni]   'peanut'
     /u/   ['triβu]   'tribe'
     /ú/   [ɲan'du]   'rhea'

(8) /e/   ['kaβle]   'cable'
     /é/   [be'βe]   'baby'

1.1.2 Terminal Elements in Diminutive Formation

In diminutive formation, TEs are deleted before affixation (9a); as opposed to base elements which, as Colina (2003) points out, are retained (9c). As previously argued, final /e/ behaves as a base element (9d) rather than a TE (i.e., it is not deleted before the diminutive allomorph is affixed).

In Spanish, all diminutives have a final /a/ and /o/ affixed to the diminutive allomorph. For words that do not have a TE, this final segment agrees with the gender of the word: final /a/ for feminine and final /o/ for masculine. However, words that do have a TE do not follow this pattern; rather they attach to the allomorph the same TE that was previously attached to the stem, regardless of the gender of the word (Colina, 2003; Harris, 1969), as seen in (9b).

(9) (a)   ['kas-a]   'house'   →   [ka'sita]
     (b)   ['map-a]   'map, masc.'   →   [ma'pita]   *[ma'pito]
     (c)   [ma'ni]   'peanut, masc.'   →   [mani'sito]
     (d)   ['kaβle]   'cable, masc'   →   [kaβle'sito]

1.2 Target Dialect

Although diminutive formation is highly productive in Spanish, it is not a uniform process across all dialects. Prieto (1992) points this out in her analysis where she compares diminutives from Bolivian and Peninsular Spanish (e.g. [o'tel] 'hotel' → [otel'sito] (Bolivia) vs. [ote'lito] (Peninsular)). She adds that "other diminutive forms such as *-ill, -cill, -ecill, -in, -cin, -ecin*, and *-ic, -cic, -ecic* are generally used in the same manner" (171), as *-it, -cit, -ecit* are used in the dialect used in the present study. To obtain a clear picture, this paper focuses only on one dialect, Porteño Spanish, and consequently on only one set of diminutive forms: *-it, -cit*, and *-ecit*.

Porteño Spanish is the dialect spoken mainly in the capital of Argentina, Buenos Aires. Approximately 20,000,000 inhabitants of Buenos Aires and Greater Buenos Aires as well as from a few neighboring cities in Uruguay across the De la Plata River speak this dialect.

1.3 Maximum Entropy Model

A Maximum Entropy (hereafter, MaxEnt) grammar consists of a set of numerically weighted constraints calculated based on the percentage of occurrence of each output for a specific input (Martin, 2007). The goal of this model is not only to account for the favorite candidate, but also to express the ambivalence that exists in a set of candidates or outputs. The method has been previously applied by Goldwater and Johnson (2003), and Hayes and Wilson (2008). Goldwater and Johnson (2003) explain that "[t]his model is probabilistic, making it resistant to noise, and seeks to reproduce the distribution of output forms in a training corpus, thus modeling free variation. Like Optimality Theory, the MaxEnt model treats constraints as additive, thus accounting for cumulativity effects" (2).[4] The constraints' weights are assigned based on the Real Frequency (i.e., the number of occurrences of the candidates of a particular input) and the Real Proportion (i.e., its percentage of occurrence within each input), which in turn yields a predicted percentage of occurrence (Predicted Proportion).[5]

The goal is to generate a grammar whose weighted constraints yield a Predicted Proportion as close as possible to the Real Proportion; thus, accounting for as much variation found in the data as possible. Appendix B illustrates how the model calculates the Predicted Proportion.

The software used in this project was OTsoft version 2.3 (Hayes et al., 2008), which was developed in the Linguistics Department at UCLA. This software uses the statistical method of maximum entropy to develop a grammar based on constraints that receive a specific weight which accounts for frequencies of variants.

2. METHODOLOGY

2.1 Participants

The test subjects for this study consisted of three male and three female native speakers of Porteño Spanish from Buenos Aires, Argentina. Their ages ranged between 28 and 62 years old. To ensure there would be little or no dialectal variation among them, the speakers chosen had similar level of education (at least some college or graduated from college), had similar socioeconomic status (upper middle class), and grew up and resided in the same area of the city (Northern Buenos Aires). Thus, their speech can be considered characteristic of an educated Porteño speaker.

2.2 Stimuli

The stimuli consisted of approximately 650 words including nouns, adjectives, and adverbs, with all the possible phonemic endings: the five vowel phonemes (both stressed and unstressed) and the thirteen consonant phonemes present in word-final position according to Spanish phonotactics (Harris, 1969).[6] The words were collected from two reverse Spanish dictionaries, Stahl and Scavnicky (1973) and Bosque and Pérez Fernández (1987). The list had the words in random order to obtain a more natural production and to avoid the recognition of patterns that could lead the consultants to follow a pattern as opposed to their own instinct.

2.3 Procedure

Participants were involved in one production task. A native speaker of their same dialect produced the non-diminutive form of each word and they were asked to produce the diminutive form of the word once. As previously mentioned, words were given in random order, and all participants were exposed to the same ordering. The entire experiment lasted approximately sixty minutes per participant, and they were recorded in Buenos Aires, Argentina, in September 2007, using an iPod 4th generation.

After the data was gathered, the words were entered into a spreadsheet to facilitate sorting according to: (1) last phoneme, (2) last two phonemes, (3) number of syllables in casual or formal speech, and (4) allomorph used in each case. A second spreadsheet grouped all of the outputs for each input by candidates. Each candidate's absolute value of occurrence was reflected as the "Real Frequency," and its percentage of occurrence in relation to the other candidates of the same input was noted as the "Real Proportion." There was also a large number of "no response" answers that were not taken into consideration when analyzing the percentage of occurrence of each allomorph.

3. Results

3.1 Final Vowels

After analyzing vowel-final words preceded by a consonant and by another vowel or a glide, it was found that although the treatment of the segment preceding the allomorph might be different in each case (deletion or retention), the allomorphs are selected based on the final segment, and sometimes on the number of syllables; thus, the second to last segment has no influence on the allomorph selection. To account for the difference between deletion or retention of the last segment, when this segment is not a TE, phonological processes re-apply after the morphological process has been completed. This paper assumes that the input is morphologically treated, which yields an output that in turn becomes the input for the phonological process, which is what ultimately becomes the surface representation as illustrated in figure 1 (Kiparsky, 1982, p. 132).

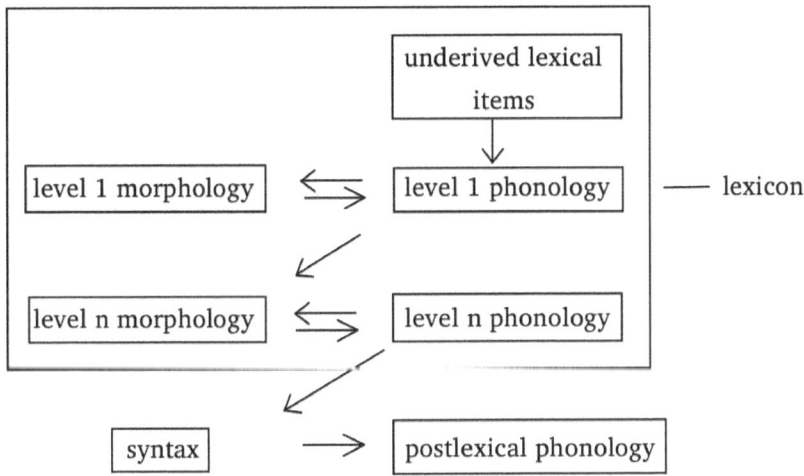

Figure 1. Lexical Phonology Model

The following table shows an overview of all the possible final segments and the allomorph most frequently selected by each one in Spanish diminutives.[7]

TABLE 1. **Overview of Final Vowels and the Allomorph Most Frequently Selected**

- it				- sit			
Phoneme	Word	Diminutive	Gloss	Phoneme	Word	Diminutive	Gloss
/a/	['maɾka]	[maɾ'kita]	mark	/e/	['kaβle]	[kaβle'sito]	cable
/o/	['fweɣo]	[fwe'ɣito]	fire	/i/	['bondi]	[bondi'sito]	bus
				/á/	[t͡ʃiɾi'pa]	[t͡ʃiɾipa'sito]	diaper
				/ó/	[boŋ'go]	[bongo'sito]	bongo
				/é/	[ka'fe]	[kafe'sito]	coffee
				/í/	[ma'ni]	[mani'sito]	peanut
				/ú/	[ɲan'du]	[ɲandu'sito]	rhea

The final segments from the previous table can be regrouped into three categories for a clear analysis of the results: final terminal elements (i.e., /a/ and /o/), final unstressed base elements (i.e., /e/ and /i/), and final stressed base elements (i.e., /á/, /ó/, /é/, /í/, and /ú/).

3.1.1 Final Terminal Elements

When analyzing TEs, the most frequently used or *winning* candidate, with 90% occurrence, is that which deletes the TE and attaches the allomorph *-it* (e.g. ['maɾka] 'mark' → [maɾ'kita]).[8] Jaeggli (1980) shows in his work reflecting the Paraguayan Spanish dialect that final /a/ and /o/ take *-it*; however, he mentions that this occurs only for words with three or more syllables, and shorter words take *-esit* (e.g. ['sawɾjo] 'saurian' → [sawɾje'sito]), which is not the case in Porteño Spanish, where ['sawɾjo] → [saw'ɾito].

3.1.2 Final Unstressed Base Elements

In table 1, final /e/ and /i/ take *-sit* as the main allomorph; however, the generalization for these endings is imperfect since not all the consultants agreed as to which allomorph to affix. Moreover, it is possible to observe a difference in the percentage of generalizations between words with two or fewer syllables and those with three or more syllables. As Jaeggli (1980) points out, "the syllable length of the base is undoubtedly one of the determining factors" in selecting the allomorph (143).

3.1.2.1 MONO OR DISYLLABIC WORDS

For base elements in words with two or fewer syllables, the winning candidate, with approximately 85% occurrence, is that which retains the base element and attaches the allomorph *-sit* (e.g. ['kaβle] 'cable'→ [kaβle'sito]). In addition, both inputs (i.e. X+/e/ and X+/i/) have a second candidate with an approximate 10% occurrence, where the base element is deleted and *-it* is affixed (e.g. ['ʃeɾsei] 'jersey' → [ʃeɾse'ito]). Prieto (1992) observes in her work that disyllabic words ending in unstressed /e/ take *-it* as the allomorph; however, for final /i/ (regardless of the number of syllables in the word), she states that "the possible diminutive forms are very inconsistent across speakers" (174).

3.1.2.2 TRISYLLABIC OR LONGER WORDS

For base elements in words with three or more syllables, the winning candidate is that which retains the base element and attaches the allomorph *-sit*, just as for words with two or less syllables. However, here the winner obtains only an average of 60% of occurrence (e.g. [pexe'rej] 'mackrel' → [pexerej'sito]), with second place for deleted final vowel with attachment of *-it* allomorph at 40% occurrence (e.g. [de'saɣwe] 'drainpipe' → [desa'ɣwito]).[9]

3.1.3 Final Stressed Vowel

Fluctuating between 76% and 94% of occurrence, the most frequent winning candidate for all final stressed vowels is that which does not delete the base element and attaches -*sit* as the allomorph (e.g. [ka'fe] 'coffee' → [kafe'sito], with 94.1%); the selection of this allomorph has been previously indicated by Prieto (1992).

Within this category of final stressed vowel, a peculiar phenomenon was observed. Words that are common amongst speakers and evoke certain endearment (shown in 10) do not always follow the general pattern of attaching -*sit*, and they affix the "simpler" form -*it*. When the consultants were asked to give the diminutive form of words and probably not thinking about their meaning, but rather thinking of them as a string of sounds, they would follow the general pattern and attach -*sit*. However, when they used the same words in casual speech, when they were not aware they were forming diminutives, the informants would use the form with -*it*.[10]

(10)

		Casual Form	Elicited Form
[be'βe]	'baby'	[be'βito]	[beβe'sito]
[ma'ma]	'mom'	[ma'mita]	[mama'sita]
[pa'pa]	'dad'	[pa'pito]	[papa'sito]

3.2 Final Consonants

The following table gives an overview of all of the possible final segments and the allomorph selected by each one.[11]

TABLE 2. **Overview of Final Consonants and the Allomorph Most Frequently Selected**

- it				- sit			
Phoneme	Word	Diminutive	Gloss	Phoneme	Word	Diminutive	Gloss
x	[re'lox]	[relo'xito]	watch	b	[bao'βaβ]	[baoβaβ'sito]	tree
l	[pin'sel]	[pinse'lito]	brush	d	[ber'ðað]	[berðað'sita]	truth
				k	[bis'tek]	[bistek'sito]	steak
				m	['alβum]	[alβum'sito]	album
				n	[xa'βon]	[xaβon'sito]	soap
				ɾ	[ta'ʃeɾ]	[taʃeɾ'sito]	workshop
				s	[in'gles]	[ingles-'sito][12]	English

The output given here for final /s/ is an intermediate step between the underlying representation (UR) and the surface representation (SR) because the phonological processes of /e/ epenthesis or /s/ deletion will modify this output before it becomes the SR that a speaker normally outputs (where, [ingles-'sito] → [ingle-'sito]), as figure 1 previously showed. This process is later analyzed in the Phonology section of this paper. Furthermore, the consonants from the previous table will be grouped into two categories for a clear analysis of the results: consonants that normally attach -*sit* and consonants that normally attach -*it*.

3.2.1 Final Consonants that Normally Attach -sit

The percentage of occurrence of -*sit* for words ending in /b/, /d/, /k/, /m/, /n/, and /r/ fluctuates between 71% and 95%. The highest percentages (i.e., /n/ and /r/ with over 90%) agree with the data presented by Jaeggli (1980) and Prieto (1992). Jaeggli (1980) also states that final /d/ takes -*sit*; however, when he presents the data, he is not certain of that diminutive formation:

"ciudad   ?ciudadsita   'city'" (Jaeggli, 1980, 144)

This uncertainty is reflected in the data presented here by a lower percentage of occurrence of that allomorph (71%). On the other hand, the previous works on diminutives (Jaeggli, 1980; Crowhurst, 1992; Harris, 1992 & 1994; Prieto,1992; and Colina, 2003) do not account for final /b/, /k/ or /m/.

3.2.1.1 FINAL /s/

A first glance at the examples, (11) and (12a), shows that words with final /s/ take both –*sit* and –*esit* as the allomorph.

(11)   [in'gles]   'English'   [ingle'sito]

(12) (a)   ['lus]   'light'   [luse'sita]
    (b)   [traɣa'lus]   'skylight'   [traɣaluse'sita]

However, the analysis for this case is much deeper as phonology plays an important role in the formation of diminutives for words ending in /s/.

As previously mentioned in the introduction of this paper, -*esit* is not considered an allomorph on its own; rather it is the -*sit* allomorph with an epenthesized /e/, thus yielding all the allomorphs for the phoneme /s/ to be -*sit*, which is indeed what the data in this study showed (e.g. [in'gles] 'English' → [ingles'sito]).

After the allomorph -*sit* is affixed, an intermediate output is formed which has two options. If the word's stem has two or more syllables, it undergoes /s/ deletion (example 11). If the word's stem is monosyllabic, then /e/ is epenthesized (example 12a). Note that the number of syllables corresponds to the stem of the word. In compounded words, the length of the base stem is what counts; therefore, when a compounded word with a monosyllabic base forms a diminutive, an /e/ is epenthesized just as with monosyllabic words (example 12b).

One could argue that final /s/ takes two different allomorphs according to the length of the stem (-*it* and -*esit*); however, it is a much simpler approach to select only one allomorph for the /s/ final phoneme, and to follow this by the application of phonological rules that comply with the phonotactics of Spanish that prevent *[ss] from of occurring.

3.2.1.2 CONSONANT DELETION OR LENITION

As mentioned earlier, consonants do not get deleted because they form part of the base. However, examples where the final consonant was deleted were actually found in the data:

(13) [bao'βaβ]   'type of tree'   [baoβa'sito]

      [e'ðað]   'age'   [eða'sita]

      [ko'ɲak]   'cognac'   [koɲa'sito]

This deletion was consistent with a dialectal deletion or lenition that is applied across the board to final stops in Porteño Spanish (and other Spanish dialects). Furthermore, this deletion takes place after the morphological process has occurred because the allomorph chosen correlates to the one normally chosen by the given consonant, as opposed to the one that the segment preceding the final stop would choose. Thus,

(14) [bao'βaβ]   'type of tree'   [baoβaβ'sito]   →   [baoβa'sito]

      [e'ðað]   'age'   [eðað'sita]   →   [eða'sita]

      [ko'ɲak]   'cognac'   [koɲak'sito]   →   [koɲa'sito]

These outputs constrast with the ones that would have resulted from having the deletion process occur before the affixation (i.e., instead of attaching the allomorph to a final consonant, /a/ would have been

the final phoneme the allomorph would have been attached to, resulting in a deletion of the /a/ after the attachment of the allomorph -*it*):

(15) [bao'βaβ]   'type of tree'   [bao'βa]   →   *[bao'βito]

      [e'ðað]   'age'   [e'ða]   →   *[e'ðita]

      [ko'ɲak]   'cognac'   [ko'ɲa]   →   *[ko'ɲito]

3.2.2 Final Consonants that Normally Attach -it

The only two final consonants that select -*it* as their allomorph instead
of -*sit* are /x/ and /l/. Final /x/ was not discussed in the literature analyzed. On the other hand, Jaeggli (1980) does examine final /l/ and he
comes to a different conclusion. He proposes that final /l/ takes -*sit*
for monosyllables and -*it* for words with two or more syllables (16).
However, the data obtained from Porteño Spanish does not follow
this pattern or any other particular pattern of distinction between -*sit*
and -*it*. Thus, the data collected in some cases follows Jaeggli's (1980)
proposal (as in example 16 [kana'lito] and example 17 [mjel'sita]),
but not consistently (as in example 16 [ma'lito]).

(16)   Jaeggli's proposal   Porteño Spanish

    ['mal]   'bad'   [mal'sito]   [ma'lito]

    [ka'nal]   'channel'   [kana'lito]   [kana'lito]

(17)   Jaeggli's proposal   Porteño Spanish

    ['mjel]   'honey'   [mjel'sita]   [mjel'sita]

3.3 Phonology

The following phonological processes account for the treatment of
stem final diphthongs and final /s/ after morphology has applied.
They are evaluated using Maximum Entropy as the previous
morphology sections.

3.3.1 Diphthong Phonology

3.3.1.1 SECONDARY STRESS

The process of secondary stress formation is summarized in table 3.
The two constraints involved in the process are:

1) **Max-'σ** prevents complete deletion of stress from a syllable.
This does not imply changing the stress from primary to secondary.
This constraint is violated when a syllable is deleted or when stress is
removed from a syllable.

2) *'σ-'σ implies that it is illegal to have two contiguous primary stresses in a word. This constraint is violated when a morpheme that carries primary stress is affixed in a word next to the primary stressed syllable without altering the value of this stress to secondary stress; thus making the change from primary to secondary stress on the unaffixed word, the best candidate (e.g. [[kan'sjon] 'song' → [kansjon'sita]).

TABLE 3. **Insertion of *'σ-'σ Constraint**

Input	Candidate	Real Freq.	Real prop.	Pred. prop.	Max-'σ	*'σ-'σ
				Weights:	3.587	18.28
'σ 'σ	,σ 'σ	289	0.973	0.973		
'σ 'σ	Ø 'σ	8	0.027	0.027	1	
'σ 'σ	'σ 'σ	0	0	0		1

3.3.1.2 GLIDE MERGE

The data collected showed that when the *-it* suffix was attached to a word ending in a front glide, both sounds would merge into one instead of remaining as a diphthong. To account for this process, a new constraint was created:

*Merge GV prevents assimilation and merge of a glide and a contiguous vowel when both have the same backness. The environment that triggers such a merge is generated every time the allomorph *-it* is attached to a word that ends in diphthong formed with a front glide and a terminal element, because once the TE drops, the glide will tend to merge with the attached vowel. In Porteño Spanish, such is the case of:

(18) ['tapja]   'wall'   [ta'pjita] →   [ta'pita]

However, as Colina (2003) points out, other dialects do not undergo this merge:

(19) ['tapja]   'wall'   [tapje'sita]   (Peninsular Spanish)

3.3.2 *Final /s/ Phonology*

For the purposes of the phonological process, words ending in /s/ were separated into two subsets: monosyllables (e.g. ['lus] 'light') or compounds where the stems are monosyllables (e.g. [traɣa'lus] 'sky-light'), and words with two or more syllables.

TABLE 4. Insertion of *Gem and Dep-V Constraints

Input	Candidate	Real Freq.	Real prop.	Pred. prop.	*Gem	Dep-V	*s + syll
				Weights:	5.62	0.155	2.279
Xssit (1 syll)	Xsesit	41	0.461	0.46		1	
Xssit (1 syll)	Xssit	0	0	0.002	1		
Xssit (1 syll)	Xsit	48	0.539	0.538			
Xssit (2+syll)	Xsesit	20	0.08	0.08		1	1
Xssit (2+syll)	Xssit	1	0.004	0.003	1		
Xssit (2+syll)	Xsit	228	0.916	0.916			

Table 4 illustrates the two processes that apply to final /s/: /e/ epenthesis, and /s/ deletion. The process of /e/ epenthesis applies to monosyllables (e.g. ['bals] 'waltz' → [balse'sito]), and the /s/ deletion applies to words with two or more syllables (e.g. [in'gles] 'English' → [ingles'sito] → [ingle'sito]). The two constraints involved in these processes are the following:

1) *Gem stands for ungrammatical geminate. Following Spanish phonotactics, this constraint does not allow consonant geminates; thus, marking as illegal the /ss/ sequence.

2) Dep-V states that every vowel in the output must have an input vowel. In this particular case, it is violated when /e/ is epenthesized to solve the geminate. However, this process is based on the fact that Spanish already shows a similar epenthesis process in the formation of plurals for final /s/ words:

(20) ['kos]   'kick, sg.'   ['koses]   'kick, pl.'

      [aβes'trus]   'ostrich, sg.'   [aβes'truses]   'ostrich, pl.'

4. CONCLUSION

Using a Maximum Entropy grammar, this paper shows a full account of the free variation found in the data set from the elicitation of diminutives from six native speakers of Porteño Spanish. A set of ten constraints (explained in detail in Appendix A) was developed in order to restrict the diminutive formation process. Additionally, the interaction of this process with phonological processes was drawn for the particular case of words ending in /s/. Furthermore, the proposed constraints and interaction with phonology achieved on average 90% accuracy when comparing the real proportion and the predicted proportion of occurrence for every candidate; thus yielding a very significant account for the variation of diminutive formation in Porteño Spanish.

Neveretheless, although it seems that all of the candidates were treated in this analysis, there is one more output that has not been studied in this paper: no response. During the elicitation process, two types of no-response were encountered: "I don't know how to form the diminutive of that word" and "That word doesn't have a diminutive." Considering the productivity of this process and that all of the words from the list could form diminutives, the next step in the analysis of diminutives would be to evaluate if speakers follow any pattern in stating which words do not allow diminutive formation; are words marked for diminutive formation? If not, how do speakers know when a noun, adjective or adverb can form a diminutive or not?

APPENDIX A: CONSTRAINTS

The following ten constraints were used to generate a Maximum Entropy grammar. Extensive informal experimentation with a variety of different constraints gave this somewhat intuitive explanation of what they do.

Co-Co (i.e., coda stays coda) prevents a coda from becoming an onset in a following syllable (e.g. [bao'βaβ] 'baobab tree' → [baoβaβ'sito]). Considering that final consonants do not delete, every time the allomorph *-it* is attached, this constraint is violated (e.g. ['kluβ] 'club' → [klu'βito]). This constraint is based on Stephenson's proposal of a constraint for classical OT that she calls *Ident (Base – dim) Syl-Pos* where "segments in the diminutive must have the same syllable position (onset or rhyme) as their corresponding segments in the base" (21).

Max-baseV states that every base-vowel input must have an output correspondent (i.e., do not delete a vowel that is a base element). As mentioned in the first section of this paper, TEs do not form part of the base, and they delete when an allomorph is affixed. Therefore, rather than having a constraint such as Max-V that would be violated every time a vowel is deleted, to simplify the number of violations, this narrower constraint is used instead, which is violated only when a base element vowel is deleted (e.g. ['nene] 'kid' → [ne'nito]).

*Hiatus is violated every time the allomorph *-it* is attached next to a vowel, requiring a separate pronunciation of the two adjacet vowels. Hiatuses are legal sound sequences in Spanish; however, the dialect prefers not to form additional ones when attaching a suffix (e.g. [baka'lao] 'cod' → [bakalao'ito]).

*FrV-FrV (i.e., *FrontV-FrontV) prevents from having two adjacent front vowels. It targets a subset of the candidates that violate ***Hiatus**. The use of this constraint becomes apparent when looking at all final vowels together, since the percentage that final /é/ and /í/ attach *-it* to the base without final vowel deletion is much smaller than final /á/, /ó/ or /ú/ (1.5% and 0% vs. 2.3% and 15% respectively).[13]

*Stop coda prevents having a stop as a coda. Although this constraint seems to contradict Co-Co, its purpose is to differentiate between any consonant in the coda position (e.g. [kan'sjon] 'song' → [kansjon'sita]) and a stop in the coda position (e.g. [ber'ðað] 'truth' → [berðað'sita]) and account for the difference in frequency between a stop coda and a non-stop coda.

*Phon (i.e., *Phonotactics) is violated any time an illegal segment sequence is triggered. For the purposes of diminutive formation, the possible illegal sequences violated are /ds/, /ms/ and /xs/ since these sequences do not normally occur in Spanish. Its effects can be seen in the analysis of nasals, given that the candidate that violates this constraint (Xm-sit; e.g. ['alβum] 'album' → [alβum'sito]) occurs 12% less than the one that does not violate it (Xn-sit; e.g. [kan'sjon] 'song' → [kansjon'sita]), and in turn the predicted proportion of the first one is smaller than the latter. Although /ss/ is also an illegal sequence, it is not considered illegal here because the output of the morphological process still has to undergo the phonological process which remedies for that.

*5 + syll is violated when a word has five or more syllables as a consequence of suffixation. The candidates that violate it are those whose input are stems with three or more syllables with final BE and attach the allomorph *–sit*, which adds two more syllables to the stem (e.g. [pexe'rej] 'mackerel' → [pexerej'sito]). Here again there is a difference in frequency between the candidates that do not violate this constraint and those that do; for example, disyllabic words ending in /i/ that take *-sit* (e.g. ['bondi] 'bus' (slang) → [bondi'sito]) have a real proportion of occurrence of approximately 88%, as opposed to trisyllabic ones with a proportion of ocurrence of approximately 55%.

No sit is violated every time the allomorph *-sit* is attached to the stem (e.g. ['laktea] 'milky' → [laktea'sita]). Although it might seem logical to add the counterpart **No it**, when this constraint was added and run through the program, its weight was 0.00, meaning it had no influence in the grammar. On the other hand, if **No sit** were to be taken off of the grammar, all of the inputs would lose some degree of accuracy; in addition, there would be no differentiation for final {a,o} between the following three candidates: X[a/o] sit, X-it (e.g. ['marka] 'mark' → [mar'kita]), and X-sit (e.g. ['boa] 'boa' → [bo'sita]) since aside from **No sit** they do not violate any other constraint.

*ls targets the sequence /ls/. Candidates for final /l/ behave different than candidates for other inputs that, besides ***ls**, violate the same constraints (i.e., final /n/, /r/ and /s/). However, final /l/ takes *-it* as the primary allomorph (e.g. ['gol] 'goal' → [go'lito]) as opposed to the other three inputs which select *-sit* (e.g. [ta'ʃer] 'workshop' → [taʃer'sito]).

*xs takes care specifically of the violation of the sequence /xs/, previously violated by ***Phon**. However, ***Phon** alone does not account for the difference in frequency between candidates that include /xs/ and those that do not (e.g. [re'lox] 'watch' → [relox'sito], with 23.3% real proportion of occurrence). After experimenting with different more general constraints, no other constraint was found that would reflect this difference which is specifically seen when comparing final /m/ (that takes *-sit* as the allomorph, e.g. ['alβum] 'album' → [alβum'sito]) and final /x/ (that takes *-it*; e.g. [re'lox] 'watch' → [relo'xito], with 76.7% real proportion of occurrence).

APPENDIX B: CANDIDATES AND INPUTS

The following tables combine all of the inputs and candidates with the constraints that apply in each particular case. Notice that the constraints obtain their weights as a result of the analysis of all the inputs, their respective candidates and their frequencies; thus interacting with each other even if they do not affect the same candidate. Phonological constraints are not included since they are applied after the morphological process that involves these constraints, and only to a subset of the inputs.

TABLE B.1. Final Unstressed Vowels

Input	Candidate	Example	*Phonotactics	*5+syll	*Stop coda	*FrV FrV	No sit	*xs	*ls	*Hiatus	Max-baseV	Co-Co	Pred. prop.	Real prop.	Real Freq.
Weights:			0.85	1.28	1.76	3.17	3.17	3.60	3.81	4.52	4.88	6.41			
X{a/o}	X-it	[ˈmarka] → [marˈkita] 'mark'											0.913	0.908	836
X{a/o}	X{a/o}-sit	[ˈlaktea] → [lakteaˈsita] 'milky'					1						0.039	0.053	49
X{a/o}	X{a/o}-it	[bakaˈlao] → [bakalaoˈito] 'cod'								1			0.010	0.026	24
X{a/o}	X-sit	[ˈboa] → [boˈsita] 'boa'					1						0.039	0.013	12
Xe2	Xe-sit	[ˈkaβle] → [kaβleˈsito] 'cable'					1						0.834	0.840	68
Xe2	X-it	[ˈnene] → [neˈnito] 'kid'									1		0.150	0.160	13
Xe2	Xe-it					1				1			0.009	0	0
Xe2	X-sit						1				1		0.006	0	0
Xi2	Xi-sit	[bondi] → [bondiˈsito] 'bus'					1						0.834	0.880	88
Xi2	X-it	[ˈʃersei] → [ʃerseˈito] 'jersey'									1		0.150	0.110	11
Xi2	Xi-it	[kaˈði] → [kaˈðito] 'caddy'				1				1			0.009	0.010	1
Xi2	X-sit						1				1		0.006	0	0
Xe3	Xe-sit	[eroe] → [eroeˈsito] 'hero'		1			1						0.584	0.630	29
Xe3	X-it	[deˈsaɣwe] → [desaˈɣwito] 'drainpipe'									1		0.377	0.370	17
Xe3	Xe-it					1				1			0.023	0	0
Xe3	X-sit						1				1		0.016	0	0
Xi3	Xi-sit	[pexeˈrej] → [pexerejˈsito] 'mackrel'		1			1						0.584	0.552	37
Xi3	X-it	[brokoli] → [brokoˈlito] 'broccoli'									1		0.377	0.448	30
Xi3	Xi-it					1				1			0.023	0	0
Xi3	X-sit						1				1		0.016	0	0

TABLE B.2. Final Stressed Vowels

Input	Candidate	*Phonotactics	*5+syll	*Stop coda	*FrV FrV	No sit	*xs	*ls	*Hiatus	Max-baseV	Co-Co	Pred. prop.	Real prop.	Real Freq.	Example
X{á/ó}	X{á/ó}-sit					1						0.692	0.773	68	[tʃiˈripa] → [tʃiripaˈsito] 'cloth diaper'
X{á/ó}	X-it									1		0.124	0.205	18	[maˈma] → [maˈmita] 'mom'
X{á/ó}	X{á/ó}-it								1			0.178	0.023	2	[noˈʃo] → [noʃoˈito] 'type of liqueur'
X{á/ó}	X-sit	1				1				1		0.005	0	0	
Xé	Xé-sit					1						0.834	0.941	64	[kaˈfe] → [kafeˈsito] 'coffee'
Xé	X-it									1		0.150	0.044	3	[beˈβe] → [beˈβito] 'baby'
Xé	Xé-it				1				1			0.009	0.015	1	[kiˈtʃe] → [kitʃeˈito] 'Guatemalan indians'
Xé	X-sit	1				1				1		0.006	0	0	
Xi	Xi-sit					1						0.834	0.758	97	[maˈni] → [maniˈsito] 'peanut'
Xi	X-it									1		0.150	0.211	27	[karmeˈsi] → [karmeˈsito] 'crimson'
Xi	Xi-it				1				1			0.009	0.031	4	[esˈki] → [eskiˈito] 'ski'
Xi	X-sit	1				1				1		0.006	0	0	
Xú	Xú-sit					1						0.692	0.825	33	[nanˈdu] → [nanduˈsito] 'rhea'
Xú	Xú-it								1			0.178	0.150	6	[alaˈxu] → [alaxuˈito] 'type of candy'
Xú	X-it									1		0.124	0.025	1	[fuˈfu] → [fuˈfito] 'type of dish'
Xú	X-sit	1				1				1		0.005	0	0	

TABLE B.3. Final Consonants

Example	*Phonotactics	*5+syll	*Stop coda	*FrV FrV	No sit	*xs	*ls	*Hiatus	Max-baseV	Co-Co	Pred. prop.	Real prop.	Real Freq.	Candidate	Input
[baoˈβaβ] → [baoβaβˈsito] 'type of tree'			1		1						0.815	0.737	14	Xb-sit	Xb
[kluβ] → [kluˈβito] 'gym'	1									1	0.185	0.263	5	Xb-it	Xb
[berˈðað] → [berðaðˈsita] 'truth'			1		1					1	0.654	0.708	63	Xd-sit	Xd
[eˈðað] → [eðaˈðita] 'age'			1							1	0.346	0.292	26	Xd-it	Xd
[kaʃak] → [kaʃakˈsito] 'kayak'			1		1						0.815	0.710	22	Xk-sit	Xk
[bisˈtek] → [bisteˈkito] 'steak'										1	0.185	0.290	9	Xk-it	Xk
[alβum] → [alβumˈsito] 'album'	1				1						0.917	0.824	42	Xm-sit	Xm
[isˈlam] → [islaˈmito] 'islam'										1	0.083	0.176	9	Xm-it	Xm
[kanˈsjon] → [kansjonˈsita] 'song'					1						0.963	0.946	157	Xn-sit	Xn
[bwen] → [bweˈnito] 'good, masc'										1	0.037	0.054	9	Xn-it	Xn
[taˈʃer] → [taʃerˈsito] 'workshop'					1						0.963	0.924	121	Xr-sit	Xr
[seˈɲor] → [seɲoˈrito] 'gentleman'										1	0.037	0.076	10	Xr-it	Xr
[inˈgles] → [inglesˈsito] 'English'					1						0.963	1.000	338	Xs-sit	Xs
										1	0.037	0	0	Xs-it	Xs
[gol] → [goˈlito] 'goal'										1	0.638	0.638	139	Xl-it	Xl
[alβaˈɲil] → [alβaɲilˈsito] 'construction worker'					1		1				0.362	0.362	79	Xl-sit	Xl
[reˈlox] → [reloˈxito] 'watch'						1				1	0.767	0.767	33	Xx-it	Xx
[reˈlox] → [reloxˈsito] 'watch'	1				1						0.233	0.233	10	Xx-sit	Xx

Appendix C: Maximum Entropy Model

The following tables illustrate how the Maximum Entropy model calculates the Predicted Proportion.

Table 1 shows the outputs for a specific input and the constraints they violate. As in classic Optimality Theory (OT) (Prince & Smolensky, 1993), one must indicate the number of times that each constraint is violated (i.e., "1" in this table corresponds to one ungrammatical * in OT). A crucial element in this model is the Real Frequency, which is the number of times that each output happens per input for a specific set of data; this is the main difference between this model and classic OT, since here free variation is accounted for. After learning, the program assigns a number (weight) to each constraint (Cons.).

Table 1. Outputs and violations per constraint

			Cons. 1	Cons. 2	Cons. 3	Cons. 4
		Weights:	5.08	3.22	1.02	3.68
Input	Output 1		1	1		
	Output 2				1	1
	Output 3		1		1	

Table 2 shows the first step of the process, which is to multiply each weight by the number of violations per output.

Table 2. Weighted violations

		Cons. 1	Cons. 2	Cons. 3	Cons. 4
Input	Output 1	5.08	3.22		
	Output 2			1.02	3.68
	Output 3	5.08		1.02	

Table 3 shows, in the column on the far right, the sum of the penalties for each output.

Table 3. Penalties per input

		Cons. 1	Cons. 2	Cons. 3	Cons. 4	SUM
Input	Output 1	5.08	3.22			8.30
	Output 2			1.02	3.68	4.70
	Output 3	5.08		1.02		6.10

Table 4 shows the result of taking the number e to the minus sum previously calculated in the right column.

Table 4. e to the minus sum

		Cons. 1	Cons. 2	Cons. 3	Cons. 4	e - SUM
Input	Output 1	5.08	3.22			2.485E-04
	Output 2			1.02	3.68	9.095E-03
	Output 3	5.08		1.02		2.243E-03

Table 5 shows (at the bottom of the right column) the result of adding the values calculated in table 4.

TABLE 5. Addition of Table 4

		Cons. 1	Cons. 2	Cons. 3	Cons. 4	e - SUM
Input	Output 1	5.08	3.22			2.485E-04
	Output 2			1.02	3.68	9.095E-03
	Output 3	5.08		1.02		2.243E-03
					TOTAL	1.159E-02

Finally, table 6 shows, in the right column, the computation of the proportional share of each output compared against the real frequency (Real Fr.) on the third column from the left.

TABLE 6. Proportional Share

		Real Fr.	Cons. 1	Cons. 2	Cons. 3	Cons. 4	e - SUM	PROP.
Input	Output 1	5	5.08	3.22			2.485E-04	2.144
	Output 2	195			1.02	3.68	9.095E-03	78.473
	Output 3	51	5.08		1.02		2.243E-03	19.353
						TOTAL	1.159E-02	

The proportion obtained in the last table is the "Predicted Proportion" based on the real frequency, the violations and the weight of each constraint.

Once the Predicted Proportion (Pred. Prop.) has been calculated, the Real Frequency percentage can be compared with the Predicted Proportion percentage to determine the accuracy of the predicted values. When looking at table 7 below, output 2 was predicted to occur 79% of the time and it occurred 78% of the time, yielding a 98.7% accuracy.

TABLE 7. Comparison of Real Frequencies and Predicted Proportion

		Real Fr.	Real Fr. (%)	Pred. Prop.	Pred. Prop. (%)
Input	Output 1	5	2	2.144	2
	Output 2	195	78	78.473	79
	Output 3	51	20	19.353	19

Notes

1. Although Spanish is commonly known as a "phonetic language," meaning that the spelling reflects the phonemes in the language, there are some phonemes that can be represented by more than one character (e.g. <casa> 'house' IPA ['kasa] and <caza> 'hunt' IPA ['kasa]), and some characters represent different phonemes according to the environment (e.g. <cara> 'face' IPA ['kaɾa] and <cera> 'wax' IPA ['seɾa]). Thus, in this paper all the phonetic transcriptions will be shown in IPA, abstracting away from the language's allophones.

2. However, as Jaeggli (1980) argues, and it is shown here, -*esit* is not a separate allomorph, rather the allomorph -*sit* that undergoes epenthesis of /e/. This paper further argues that the morphological process of diminutive formation interacts with the phonological process of epenthesis in specific environments.

3. Where X'e stands for any word that finishes in a stressed [e].

4. Optimality Theory is a linguistic model of how grammars are constructed. It proposes that observed forms of language arise from the interaction between conflicting constraints; thus modeling grammars as systems that provide mappings from inputs (underlying representations) to outputs (surface representations). For a more detailed explanation, see Prince & Smolensky (1993).

5. For a full explanation of how the Maximum Entropy Model calculates the Predicted Proportion, see Appendix C.

6. Words ending in /p/, /t/, /f/ and /g/ are not included in the analysis in this paper because they occur only in loan words that have not yet been adapted to follow Spanish phonotactics; and they do not follow any specific pattern for diminutive formation.

7. Final unstressed /u/ is not shown because there are not enough words in Spanish with this ending to be able to make a generalization based solely on the data. However, based on the behavior of final stressed /u/, which follows a similar pattern of the other two final base elements, this paper assumes that this behavior parallels for unstressed final vowels.

8. For a full account of inputs, candidates, and their interaction with constraints, see Appendix A.

9. For purposes of diminutive formation, glides /j/ and /w/ behave as the vowels /i/ and /u/.

10. Although studying diminutive formation in casual speech was not part of this project, in casual non-research related conversations the author noted these instances of diminutive formation as illustrated in example 10, which were quite salient as unnatural Porteño Spanish during the elicitation process.

11. As mentioned earlier, words ending in /p/, /t/, /f/ and /g/ are not analyzed in this paper. (See Endnote 6)

12. Following Kiparsky's model previously discussed, this paper assumes that the input is morphologically treated, which yields an output that in turn becomes the input for the phonological process, which is what ultimately becomes the surface representation. Therefore, the case of final /s/ will be first analyzed in terms of the morphological process and a phonological process will later account for the degemination process (see section 3.3.2).

13. See Appendix B, Table B.2 for final stressed vowels.

Works Cited

Bosque, Ignacio and Manuel Pérez Fernández. *Diccionario inverso de la lengua española*. Madrid: Editorial Gredos, 1987. Print.

Colina, Sonia. "Diminutives in Spanish: a morpho-phonological account." *Southwest Journal of Linguistics* 22.2 (2003): 45-88. Print.

Crowhurst, Megan J. "Diminutives and augmentatives in Mexican Spanish: a prosodic analysis." *Phonology* 9 (1992): 221-253. Print.

Goldwater, Sharon and Mark Johnson. "Learning OT constraint rankings using a maximum Entropy Model." *Proceedings of the Stockholm Workshop on Variation within Optimality Theory*. Eds. J. Spenader, A. Eriksson and O. Dahl. Stockholm: Stockholm University, 2003. 111-120. Print.

Harris, James. *Spanish Phonology*. Cambridge, MA: The MIT Press, 1969. Print.

———. "The form classes of Spanish diminutives." *Yearbook of Morphology 1991* 4 (1992): 65-88. Print.

———. "The OCP, prosodic morphology and Sonoran Spanish diminutives: a reply to Crowhurst." *Phonology* 11.1 (1994): 179-190. Print.

Hayes, Bruce, Bruce Tesar, and Kie Zuraw. *OTSoft (Version 2.3)* [software]. *Department of Linguistics, UCLA*. 2003. Web. Jan. 15, 2008.

Hayes, Bruce and Colin Wilson. "A Maximum Entropy Model of phonotactics and phonotactic learning." *Linguistic Inquiry* 39 (2008): 379-440. Print.

Jaeggli, Osvaldo. "Spanish diminutives." *Contemporary Studies in Romance Language: Proceedings of the Eighth Annual Symposium on Romance Languages*. Ed. Frank Nuessel Jr. Bloomington, IN: Indiana University Linguistics Club, 1980. 142-158. Print.

Kiparsky, Paul. "From Cyclic Phonology to Lexical Phonology." *The Structure of Phonological Representations*. Eds. H. Hulst and N. Smith. Dordrecht, Holland: Foris Publishing, 1982. 131-175. Print.

Martin, Andrew T., "The evolving lexicon." Diss. University of California, Los Angeles, 2007 Web. Jan. 10, 2008.

Prieto, Pilar. "Morphophonology of the Spanish diminutives formation: a case for prosodic sensitivity." *Hispanic Linguistics* 5.1-2 (1992): 169-205. Print.

Prince, Alan and Paul Smolensky. "Optimality theory: Constraint interaction in generative grammar." *Optimality Theory in phonology*. Ed. John J. McCarthy. Malden, MA: Blackwell Publishing, 1993. Print.

Stephenson, Tamina. "Declensional-type classes in derivational morphology: Spanish diminutives revisited." *Phonology/Morphology General Papers*. MIT. 2004. Web. Feb. 13, 2008.

Stahl, Fred and Gary Scavnicky. *A Reverse Dictionary of the Spanish Language*. Urbana: University of Illinois Press, 1973. Print.

El desafío de publicar una revista transnacional y bilingüe. Una entrevista a Rose Mary Salum

Vanessa Fernández-Frey
University of California, Los Angeles

Mexicana de ascendencia libanesa, Rose Mary Salum sobresale en el ámbito literario debido a su incansable esfuerzo por fomentar vínculos entre culturas y naciones tanto en su obra como escritora y antóloga como en su revista transnacional y bilingüe *Literal: Latin American Voices.* Su obra literaria incluye tres colecciones de cuentos: *Vitrales* (1994), *Entre los espacios* (2002), *Spaces In Between* (2006); y su 'microficción' *El insomnio del arte,* que se publicará próximamente. Como antóloga, Rose Mary se ha esmerado en destacar la obra de latinoamericanos de origen árabe y judío en *Amalafa y Caligrafía: Literatura de origen árabe en América Latina* (2009) y en los *Cuentos semitas* que están por publicarse. Por su obra literaria, Rose Mary Salum ha recibido numerosos premios como "Escritora del año (2008)," otorgado por el Festival hispánico del libro de Houston, y el premio "Ana María Matute" otorgado por Torremozas. Desde Houston, Texas, Rose Mary se dedica a establecer puentes entre Latinoamérica, Canadá y los Estados Unidos a través de *Literal: Latin American Voices,* una revista trimestral que publica desde 2004.

El objetivo principal de *Literal* es ser un espacio de convergencia de varias disciplinas culturales (letras, artes visuales, política, filosofía, etc.) en el cual se promueven eminentes voces latinoamericanas. *Literal* enfoca estas voces tanto en el campo hispanoamericano como en el global. Presenta los debates del momento en y sobre Latinoamérica, pero también resalta las contribuciones que aportan intelectuales latinoamericanos a las discusiones culturales a nivel mundial. Encauza temas como el arte, el rol del intelectual, las redes sociales, el lujo, la política y la violencia. La versión impresa de *Literal* cuenta con una encuadernación elegante y un formato artístico y sofisticado que también queda plasmado en la versión digital (literalmagazine.com).

Cada tomo se centra en un tema que se estudia de modo interdisciplinario a través de las secciones de la revista: Current Events, Reflexión, Ensayo, Ficción, Poesía, Arte, Flashback, Reseñas y Entrevistas. Por su calidad, *Literal* ha recibido dos premios del CELJ (Council of Editors of Learned Journals) y tres premios Lone Star.

El 30 de abril de 2012 la organización "Motus Sodalis" y el UCLA Department of Spanish and Portuguese auspiciaron dos eventos con Rose Mary Salum. El primero fue una lectura y discusión de su cuento "Una de ellas." La conversación giró en torno al tema de la imperfección del lenguaje como modalidad de expresión; un reto al cual se enfrenta Rose Mary frecuentemente como escritora y como editora de una revista bilingüe y transnacional. Por la tarde, Rose Mary Salum profundizó en este tema durante su charla "*Literal* Magazine: Connecting Cultures Across Languages," en la cual expuso el proceso que la llevó a crear la revista, cómo ha evolucionado desde su origen y los numerosos desafíos que conlleva este ambicioso proyecto. Tras su presentación, generosamente me concedió una entrevista en la que continuamos el diálogo sobre *Literal*.

Mester: El primer tomo de *Literal* establece los propósitos de la publicación: "*Literal*: *Voces latinoamericanas* abre hoy sus páginas con un doble propósito: convertirse en un foro donde confluyan las expresiones artísticas latinoamericanas más importantes y, a la vez, abrir un espacio que permita a las nuevas voces encontrar un sitio donde expresarse" (1).[1] ¿Cómo ha cumplido *Literal* con estos propósitos iniciales en sus ocho años de publicación?

Rose Mary Salum: Ahora que retomas ese editorial publicado hace tantos años, veo con cierta satisfacción que algunos de nuestros objetivos se han cumplido. La intención era abrir un espacio donde las producciones artísticas confluyeran, provocar un diálogo que asumiera la existencia de otras lenguas, su cercanía y la necesidad de interactuar entre sí. En un mundo globalizado y en un país como Estados Unidos, el cual a diario se nutre de inmigrantes, un espacio así era necesario. Es cierto, hemos publicado a escritores jóvenes, o no tan conocidos—que para nuestro agrado ahora han sido reconocidos por otros medios e incluso con premios literarios—y escritores con una trayectoria bien establecida que han confiado en nosotros como uno de los pocos medios que trasciende hacia otras lenguas y otras geografías. Pero aún falta mucho terreno por recorrer. A pesar de mi optimismo, ocho años en la vida de una revista es poco tiempo. Esperemos poder llegar a cumplir otros tantos más.

M: ¿Podrías dar ejemplos de algunos de los escritores antes no tan reconocidos que se publicaron en *Literal*? ¿Entre los escritores con carrera establecida, hay alguno/a que quisieras destacar? ¿Por qué?

RMS: Un ejemplo concreto sucedió cuando estaba reuniendo la antología de escritores de ascendencia árabe para el *Hostos Review*. Encontré a un joven escritor muy talentoso, Rodrigo Hasbun. En el 2009 publicamos un cuento de su autoría y posteriormente un texto breve sobre uno de los temas que abordamos en *Literal*. Fue muy grato para nosotros enterarnos de que su nombre se encontraba dentro de la lista de escritores jóvenes que *Granta* publicó el año pasado. Claro, el mérito pertenece únicamente al autor, pero el hecho de saber que "tenemos buen ojo" nos hace pensar que vamos por buen camino. En el caso de la sección de arte por ejemplo, publicamos a Cara Barer, una fotógrafa poco conocida en Latinoamérica. Después de haberla publicado en *Literal*, recibió algunas invitaciones a exponer. Entre ellas, una que llegó desde Venezuela. La directora de la librería El Buscón me escribió para que por mi conducto, entregara la invitación a la artista para exponer en su librería de Caracas.

Asimismo, en los comienzos de *Literal*, publicamos a Gioconda Belli, una poeta más conocida en Estados Unidos y CentroAmérica que en México. Ella, así como Sandra Cisneros y Gonzalo Rojas, confiaron en nosotros entregándonos material que difícilmente hubiéramos soñado con publicar. Evidentemente allí radica la generosidad de los grandes cuando apoyan proyectos jóvenes como entonces era *Literal*. Hace cuatro años Gioconda Belli fue reconocida con el premio Sor Juana Inés de la Cruz, cuya ceremonia se lleva a cabo en la Feria del libro de Guadalajara. El caso de los intelectuales ha sido aún más notorio. Tal es el caso de Tony Judt, a quien en su momento le interesó la idea de ser traducido al español. Mark Lilla es otro que ha confiado en nosotros. En el caso específico de Latinoamérica, hemos recibido la misma respuesta de Roger Bartra, Mario Vargas Llosa, de Carlos Monsiváis y Carlos Fuentes cuando aún estaban entre nosotros. Así podría continuar mencionando ejemplos específicos. En ese sentido, me siento muy agradecida por la confianza de la que hemos sido objeto.

M: ¿Cómo corresponde el título de la revista a su propósito? ¿Por qué "Literal"? ¿Por qué decidiste publicar el subtítulo "Latin American Voices" en inglés?

RMS: Por varias razones. La primera es porque yo buscaba un título que pudiera leerse en ambos idiomas (español e inglés), es decir, que al primer golpe de vista, un lector entendiera el título y pudiera acceder a la publicación. Quería evitar que un lector dejara de serlo por no poder acceder a lo elemental. Escribí una larga lista de nombres de los cuales saqué Literal. Debo admitir mi debilidad por las palabras con la letra L; me parecen muy musicales, de allí que me inclinara por ese nombre. La segunda razón del título se debe a que provocaba un juego de significados y eso me gustaba. En un mundo posmoderno nada, o casi nada, puede ser literal. Con respecto al subtítulo, sentí la necesidad de recalcar que si bien existen muchas publicaciones internacionales en el mercado, pocas encuentran su anclaje en lo latinoamericano. Independientemente de que nuestra mirada incluya producciones internacionales, siempre, en todo momento, la presencia de los autores o los artistas latinos ha estado y estará garantizada. Por último, me preguntas por qué el subtítulo va en inglés. La razón es porque queríamos incursionar en el mundo angloparlante y un guiño de esta naturaleza era un buen comienzo.

M: ¿Podrías discutir un poco más respecto a qué te refieres con "incursionar en el mundo angloparlante"?

RMS: Me refiero específicamente a la introducción de textos de intelectuales y escritores latinoamericanos en el mundo angloparlante. En el artículo que escribí para el MLA, explicaba lo difícil que es Estados Unidos para leer traducciones. Desafortunadamente es un círculo vicioso: los editores no publican material de otros países porque no existen los consumidores y los lectores no leen traducciones porque los editores no las publican. Por si fuera poco, solo en círculos muy selectos se está al día de las producciones latinoamericanas. Los demás aún piensan que seguimos en el Boom y cualquier cosa que parezca venir de Latinoamérica se le relaciona automáticamente con este movimiento (lo digo por experiencia propia) o, en el caso del arte, con los muralistas. Eso sin mencionar que éste es un país que promueve muy poco el bilingüismo. Así, todo lo que no viene en su propio idioma, simplemente se ignora o se rechaza. Dicho esto, un subtítulo en inglés haría gran diferencia para una publicación tan joven.

M: ¿Por qué entiendes que los propósitos de *Literal* se pueden llevar a cabo mejor a través de una publicación bilingüe? ¿Cuál es la importancia de una publicación bilingüe que se distribuye en México, los Estados Unidos y el Canadá?

RMS: Porque como una vez lo escribió una de nuestras lectoras: "Soy cuarta generación mexicana en Estados Unidos, no hablo español y mi único lazo a mis raíces es *Literal*." Y sin embargo, este punto que tocas es uno muy vulnerable porque algunos lectores y la gente que ha querido trabajar con la revista, pregunta si no valdría la pena dejar la revista solo en español. Cuando recibimos el apoyo de "Edumndo Valadés a revistas independientes," la única crítica que recibimos fue la de no tener suficiente contenido en español. Mientras me decían esto, yo pensaba que eso mismo me decían nuestros lectores angloparlantes: "There are not enough articles in English." La página web de la revista nos ha ayudado mucho a mitigar este problema.

Ahora bien, *Literal* se mueve en un espacio atípico donde la tensión se crea justamente a través de la lengua. Definitivamente me parece muy tentador publicar solo en español, sin embargo, sería una falta de visión hacerlo de este modo. Por lo menos en estos momentos. *Literal* nació dentro de este espacio geográfico y es producto de su entorno. El formato bilingüe nos permite acceder a ambos mundos y lograr esa conexión entre culturas. No hay que olvidar que *Literal* también se mueve dentro de un mundo académico e intelectual, específicamente dentro de las universidades y de los departamentos de lenguas modernas. Muchos de los trabajos publicados se usan constantemente en las universidades, ya sea como material literario o como material para las clases de idiomas.

M: ¿Cuál es el argumento de los que te sugieren publicarla solamente en español? ¿Cómo les contestas?

RMS: Los argumentos sobran y no les falta razón. Me dicen que de dedicarnos solo a un idioma podríamos incluir más artículos o dirigirnos únicamente a los hispanos. Pero el mundo no es mono racial ni tampoco, monolingüe. Tal vez tenga este punto de vista por mi formación interdisciplinaria. Pero basta la realidad para confirmarlo. Creo más en la universalidad renacentista que en la especialización norteamericana. Pero, volviendo a la cuestión de los idiomas, mi argumento es breve: en un mundo global, una revista como *Literal* es simplemente un reflejo de su entorno.

M: ¿Podrías describir algunos de los desafíos que conlleva publicar una revista tanto bilingüe como transnacional?

RMS: ¡Son tantos! De haberlos conocido antes de iniciar este proyecto quizá no me hubiera lanzado. Entre ellos está el más obvio que es el de ejercer de forma coherente el trabajo editorial. ¿Qué puede funcionar en una revista de estas características y qué traductores son los adecuados? Es indispensable poder ofrecer textos que sean fieles a la intención y el estilo originales. Específicamente cuando hablamos de la literatura; el arte está en el decir.

Por otro lado, y ésto lo mencionó Maarten Van Delden durante la charla, ¿hasta dónde hemos llegado con las propuestas iniciales? Como decía hace unos momentos, ocho años apenas son suficientes para dar a conocer un proyecto que empezó desde cero . . . digamos que de menos cero, porque lo inicié en un país que ni siquiera era el mío. Lo comencé además sin tener antecedentes o experiencia en este medio, lo cual dificultó todo aún más. Entonces el alcance ha sido bueno pero no óptimo. Otros obstáculos a los que nos hemos enfrentado han sido la distribución, la reticencia de la gente para acostumbrarse a una revista de esta naturaleza . . . Y ¡qué decir de las redes sociales! Efectivamente, ayudan a difundir, pero en general lo que allí se trata son temas superficiales, fragmentando pensamientos ya de por sí dispersos y poco profundos. En la era del Twitter, un ensayo de Tony Judt o una entrevista con Rob Riemen pueden resultar indescifrables o difíciles de concluir.

M: Hablando de las redes sociales, *Literal*, efectivamente, tiene una página web, una página de Facebook y también tienes un blog, ¿podrías hablar un poco de cómo has mantenido a *Literal* "al tanto de los tiempos" en la era digital?

RMS: El año pasado me invitaron al Primer Encuentro de Editores de Revistas Independientes organizado por Miguel Ángel Quemain. Era un congreso de editores para editores ¿De qué podía hablar que pudiera provocar la atención de los editores? Decidí enfocar mi charla en ese mundo digital porque para nuestra buena o mala suerte, nos tocó enfrentar circunstancias sumamente distintas a las que vivieron las revistas como *Sur, Vuelta, Plural, Contemporáneos*, etc. Y es que la difusión de la cultura en publicaciones en línea ha facilitado su creación y ha hecho casi obsoleta la tarea de las revistas impresas. En aquel momento hablé de la importancia de tener presencia en el mundo real y en el mundo digital. Pienso que éste es un momento de transición y hasta que no acabe por definirse, no podremos tener una respuesta definitiva. Me gusta compararlo con la época en la que se inventó la televisión cuando el radio era el medio de comunicación por excelencia. Tal vez el radio se vio afectado por un tiempo, pero al reinventarse, reforzó su propia presencia. Ahora bien, todo indica que las publicaciones acabarán por mudarse completamente al internet. Personalmente, sigo dudándolo, al menos mientras existan lectores que se inclinen por el medio físico. En el interim, tenemos presencia en todos los medios posibles: el impreso, a través de la página web, en el Twitter, el blog y el Faccbook. La capacidad de respuesta de todos estos medios es muy buena y va creciendo a un ritmo muy rápido. Sobretodo por la cantidad de visitas y comentarios que se generan gracias a estos medios y por el número de países que nos visitan. Es innegable que una de las ventajas de la red es su capacidad de difusión. Después de la primera década del siglo XXI, una revista que pretende buscar una conexión y un diálogo entre culturas no puede limitarse únicamente al medio impreso.

M: Aunque en Latinoamérica *Literal* solo se distribuye en México, en Venezuela y el Perú, el contenido de la revista fielmente representa las "voces latinoamericanas" que promueve su título. ¿Cómo logras integrar tantas "voces latinoamericanas" en *Literal*? ¿Por qué resulta Houston una ciudad propicia para la publicación de *Literal*?

RMS: Me gusta creer, Vanessa, que Houston es un puerto de entrada a varios territorios. Su geografía permite la presencia en ambos mundos: el angloparlante y el hispanohablante. Sin embargo, debo admitir también que es aquí donde tengo casi catorce años viviendo y es desde este lugar que concebí un proyecto de esta naturaleza. Cuando me hacen esta pregunta me encuentro pensando qué fue primero, si el huevo o la gallina, porque tal vez *Literal* no hubiera sido lo mismo si la hubiera concebido desde México, o si la revista hubiese surgido de Atlanta.

En cuanto a la integración de tantas voces, quizá un poco de suerte y audacia sea todo lo que se necesite. Aunque una trayectoria de ocho años también permite que la gente confíe en uno y vea a *Literal* como un proyecto serio. Eso lo noto cuando voy a las ferias de libros o incluso a las ferias de arte. En cada viaje voy observando una ligera mejoría. Cada vez la gente ubica más a la revista y me parece que tiene que ver con el hecho de que, en la medida de lo que le es posible lograr a un proyecto independiente, tratamos de tener presencia en los eventos más importantes. Además eso nos ha ayudado a conocer a escritores e intelectuales y a establecer relaciones con ellos. No hay lugar que visite que no haga algo nuevo por la revista o trate de ponerme en contacto con alguien de ese lugar. Me parece que en el hecho de estar presente, la gente te va conociendo y aprende a confiar en tu proyecto. Por otro lado, la relación que hemos cultivado con varias universidades nos avala como un proyecto que honestamente busca la promoción de la cultura. Se ha formado una sinergía muy interesante para todas las instancias. Aquí en Houston la noción de camaradería que se ha desarrollado entre nosotros y la Univsrsidad de Rice, la Universidad de Houston, la Universidad de St. Thomas, así como con el Museum of Fine Arts, el Consulado General de México, La galería Sicardi, La galería Sonja Roesch, el Houston Institute for Culture y otras galerías de la ciudad, nos permiten colaboraciones y organizaciones de eventos culturales—como las mesas redondas, la invitación de escritores e intelectuales a la ciudad, algunas exhibiciones de arte, etc.—que de otro modo no hubiéramos podido hacer.

M: ¿Buscas nuevos espacios de distribución para *Literal*? ¿Dónde y por qué?

RMS: Vivimos en una constante búsqueda de espacios para la revista; quizá porque ésa es su propia naturaleza. El internet es una ayuda para dar a conocer los contenidos. Y las redes sociales, a pesar de mis desacuerdos, como ya lo había mencionado antes, son un paliativo. El tercer país que más lee la revista después de Estados Unidos y México es la Argentina. No hubiéramos podido llegar a ella, al resto de Sudamérica o a varios países europeos, si no fuera por el sitio en la red. Y con todo seguimos abriendo espacios—en pequeñas librerías, en universidades, galerías de arte, etc.—porque pensamos que tres países no son suficiente. Así, mandamos la revista a algunas librerías independientes de Venezuela, de Perú, ahora estamos buscando enviar la revista a Puerto Rico y estamos estudiando la manera de poder imprimir la revista en Argentina porque *Literal* tiene una cierta audiencia en aquél país pero los envíos son muy costosos. Por otro lado, empezamos a incursionar en la producción de libros y ya empezamos a contactar distribuidoras especialistas en libros.

M: En cada tomo de *Literal* destaca su cohesión temática, lo que se advierte tanto en el contenido textual como en el visual. ¿Cómo seleccionas el tema de cada tomo?

RMS: Escoger los temas es uno de los procesos que permiten la mayor creatividad en la revista. Me gusta incorporar lo que está sucediendo en el mundo para hacer cada edición más atractiva. Entonces comienza el diálogo con David, Malva y Tanya. David Medina Portillo es el jefe editorial de la revista además de ensayista y nuestro traductor estrella al español. Tanya Huntington Hyde es editora de todo el contenido en inglés además de ser la mejor traductora al inglés que conozco. Malva Flores, quien es parte del consejo editorial, es nuestra crítica más aguerrida y constantemente está subiendo los niveles de calidad de la revista. Adolfo Castañón, así como Maarten Van Delden, tienen las sugerencias más atinadas. De modo que cuando se acerca el momento de tomar una decisión comenzamos por ver qué es viable, qué es real, sobre qué tema se puede hablar efectivamente y sobre cuál sería imposible obtener colaboraciones de valor. Hay fenómenos mundiales que nos pescan entre un número y el otro y cuando queremos retomarlo ya es demasiado tarde. Otras veces nos pescan en medio de la impresión como fue el caso de Vargas Llosa y su premio Nóbel. No pudimos sacar una reflexión al respecto sino hasta la primavera siguiente. Ese es otro de los obstáculos a los que se enfrenta la revista. Sin embargo, la página web cubre de forma más actualizada lo que la versión impresa no puede. Con respecto a la sección del arte, aunque tratamos, no siempre podemos empatar a los artistas con el tema escogido. En ese sentido tampoco trato de forzar las cosas. Una de las ventajas de estar en Houston es la de tener todo el movimiento artístico que se está dando en esta ciudad porque tiene puesta su mirada en el ámbito internacional. Me refiero específicamente a que desde hace más de diez años se creó el departamento curatorial latinoamericano en el MFAH bajo la dirección de Mari Carmen Ramírez. Ella se ha dedicado a poner en el mapa internacional las producciones visuales de los artistas latinoamericanos. Desde entonces, Houston se volvió una ciudad muy importante para el arte generado en México, Centroamérica y Sudamérica. Poder darle seguimiento a este fenómeno y realizar nuestras propias propuestas resulta muy motivador para nosotros.

M: Cada tomo de *Literal* también ofrece un contenido que proviene de varias disciplinas como la política, los negocios, el arte y las letras (tanto ficción como crítica literaria). ¿Cómo logras mantener una coherencia temática e interdisciplinaria en cada tomo de la revista?

RMS: Es cierto que en los últimos años hemos incorporado otros temas además del literario y el arte visual con resultados muy favorecedores porque ha enriquecido la temática propuesta en cada trimestre. La cohesión se logra a través del tema propuesto, pero siempre con una actitud de mucha apertura. Recuerdo, por ejemplo, cuando escogimos un tema sobre la tolerancia y la fe. En ese número incluimos una conferencia que hablaba sobre respeto y tolerancia del Dalai Lama, una entrevista con Irshad Manji que trataba el tema de la fe y la intolerancia en el Islam y un cuento que reflexionaba sobre lo absurdo de las divisiones entre credos. Todo está conectado, la interdisciplina es la regla que mueve este mundo. Somos nosotros, específicamente en este país, quienes nos empeñamos en seccionar las circunstancias, la realidad.

M: En tu artículo "Editing Journals Across Languages and Cultures" narras la complejidad de tu labor como editora de una revista bilingüe ya que las traducciones que ofrece la revista no pueden ser "literales."[2] Has dicho que "Juggling languages in our pages has made us understand that language can sometimes be the agent of fate: a language determines and is determined by the structures that constrain and support it" (2). ¿Cúales son estas estructuras que restringen y apoyan al lenguaje? ¿Cómo se manifiestan en la publicación de una revista bilingüe?

RMS: Un tema que siempre me ha apasionado es el de los filósofos del lenguaje. Una lengua necesariamente determina, se impone como un fatos, un destino, porque los conductos que un idioma establece serán los canales por los que el espíritu de esa cultura se expresa y una cultura se expresa por las palabras asignadas para expresar la vida diaria, sus costumbres y su carácter. De nuevo: ¿Qué fue primero, el huevo o la gallina? Ahora bien, concretamente en la revista, este fenómeno es algo que he ido observando a lo largo de la realización de *Literal*. No sólo la sentencia se ve concretizada en las páginas de la revista, sino en la elaboración de ella. Desde cómo te aproximas a un escritor o ensayista para invitarlo a colaborar hasta el lenguaje que usará en la escritura concreta de su material. Hay materiales que recibo que simplemente no funcionan en el idioma alterno porque sé que perderán toda su fuerza e incluso su razón de ser. No se trata de la competencia de un traductor, sino de formas de canalización difícilmente traducibles.

M: Aunque *Literal* es una revista bilingüe, no todo el contenido aparece en español e inglés, ¿Por qué? ¿Qué criterio utilizas para seleccionar los textos a ser publicados en ambos idiomas?

RMS: Porque tenemos una limitación de espacio. Esa es la razón concreta. Prometemos en la revista impresa entregar los artículos en el idioma alterno si así nos lo piden nuestros lectores y lo hemos cumplido a lo largo de estos años. La página web tiene disponibles en formato bilingüe muchos de los textos que aparecieron solo en un idioma en la revista física y eso ha complementado y enriquecido nuestro trabajo. Aún quedan muchos artículos por traducir. Ahora que hemos renovado la revista online más artículos estarán disponibles en versión bilingüe.

M: Si uno de los propósitos iniciales de *Literal* era proveer un espacio en cual "confluyan . . . expresiones artísticas latinoamericanas," noto que en el presente, aunque la revista mantiene su enfoque en Latinoamérica, también trata temas globales como la primavera árabe. Más aún, el tomo más reciente conecta la primavera árabe con el movimiento mexicano "#Yo soy 132." Al respecto, ¿cómo entiendes la evolución de *Literal* desde su primer tomo? ¿Cuál es la visión que tienes para *Literal* en el presente? ¿Cómo esperas siga evolucionando *Literal*?

RMS: Personalmente, quedarme temáticamente solo en Latinoamérica era limitante. Al expresárselo a Malva, David y Tanya vi que mis propuestas tuvieron eco así que en ese sentido la transición fue fácil. Es cierto, el enfoque sigue privilegiando a los países latinos, pero también es cierto que hemos abierto las puertas a temas incluso de la economía. Pero, ¿cómo no hacerlo cuando desde el 2008 nuestra vida diaria ha sido marcada por una crisis de la que aún no salimos? ¿Cómo mantenerse indiferente a los movimientos juveniles de rebelión que nos hablan de la caducidad de las estructuras reinantes en el siglo XX? Además, en Latinoamérica la tradición intelectual permite un espacio a los temas contemporáneos que afectan la vida diaria. En ese sentido quizá en *Literal* queden residuos importantes de aquella visión universalista y comprometida de un intelectual. En el pasado hemos analizado el tema de la función de los intelectuales en varias entregas. Ellos, que van desde Rob Riemen hasta un artículo inédito de Octavio Paz, han reflexionado sobre ese tema dentro de las páginas de la revista. Sobra decir que en uno de los números más recientes acogimos abiertamente el simposio organizado por el Dr. Manuel Gutiérrez quien también sigue preguntándose y preguntando sobre la labor de un intelectual latinoamericano. Así las cosas, independientemente de la mayor o menor influencia que tengamos sobre nuestros lectores, seguiremos reflexionando sobre el mundo y sus expresiones artísticas mientras *Literal* siga publicándose.

Notas

1. Salum, Rose Mary. "Literal." Editorial. *Literal* 1 (2004): n.pag. Print.
2. ——. "Editing Journals across Languages and Cultures." *Profession* (2009): 138-144. Print.

Reviews

CORTÍNEZ, VERÓNICA y MANFRED ENGELBERT. *La tristeza de los tigres y los misterios de Raúl Ruiz*. Santiago de Chile: Editorial Cuarto Propio, 2011. 357 pp.

Raúl Ruiz forma parte de esa selecta nómina de directores tan alabados por la minoría especialista, como no suficientemente respaldados por la bibliografía académica. En el caso del director chileno, indudablemente, existen razones que excusan esa falta de eco. En primer lugar, la cantidad, diversidad genérica y difícil acceso a su obra constituyen de partida un reto para cualquier investigador del tema. Con más de un centenar de producciones (entre cortos, películas, documentales, telenovelas y series de televisión), la obra ruiciana se presenta como un mosaico difícilmente abarcable en su integridad. En segundo lugar, la recepción de su cine a través de la crítica francesa ha impuesto ciertos parámetros de lectura. Pocos investigadores han osado matizar o poner en cuestión desde el contexto hispánico ciertas concepciones ya institucionalizadas. Finalmente, en tercer lugar, el cine de Ruiz en sí ofrece retos evidentes. Su producción heteróclita se nutre de una enorme diversidad de materiales que exigen un estudioso con un perfil bastante cualificado. Los puntos de contacto de su obra con las más diversas tradiciones cinematográficas y literarias, sus preocupaciones multidisciplinares, su entronque filosófico existencialista, su rechazo a las formas de narración tradicional, su experto conocimiento técnico de la sintaxis fílmica, imponen un investigador a la altura del umbral estético de las propuestas del director. En este contexto, merece la pena saludar con entusiasmo el texto que, con tanta penetración como pasión por el cine, han preparado los profesores Verónica Cortínez y Manfred Engelbert.

A la hora de valorar el libro, merece una mención especial la voluntad de ambos autores de distanciarse de los trabajos circunstanciales, volanderos u oportunos que se han dado cita en el año de la muerte del cineasta. *La tristeza de los tigres y los misterios de Raúl Ruiz* anticipa desde su misma enigmática portada en blanco y negro un deseo de diferencia, que, mediante la internalización de su simbología, se aleja de estrategias comerciales. La imagen de una puerta en tonos grises subraya un círculo oscuro que, como ojo o mirilla, nos conduce al interior del libro. En un gesto que homenajea la imagen emblemática de *L'Île au trésor* de 1986, la portada propone de partida al lector la posibilidad de penetrar en los misterios del cine del director, a través, simbólicamente, de una progresión análoga: el lector avanzará desde la mirada atónita del niño protagonista (emblema del espectador no experto) hasta alcanzar la posición adulta del propio autor-Ruiz. La propuesta del libro, sin rechazar al lector común, aspira, por tanto, a formar un lector ruiciano, llamado a comprender las, a menudo, herméticas estrategias del director.

Como algunos críticos y reseñistas del libro ya han subrayado (Federico de Cárdenas, Carlos Flores del Pino, Waldo Rojas, Jorge Ruffinelli), el rigor documental que vertebra el volumen aporta otra de las notas distintivas del trabajo. En el contexto de los estudios sobre el director, *La tristeza de los tigres* arranca bajo una premisa funda-cional evidente: la de articular en lengua española una aproximación académica sólida y documentada a la obra de Ruiz como antes nunca se había hecho. Apartándose del carácter más o menos divulgativo de otras publicaciones, sus autores nos proponen una incursión profunda en el contexto histórico-artístico del cine chileno de fines de los 60, una indagación académica sobre los principios estéticos y filosóficos del cine de Ruiz, una invaluable ponderación acerca de las relaciones en su obra entre cine, literatura y teatro, y un nuevo y fecundo para-digma de análisis tanto de los primeros cortometrajes entre 1963 y 1967 (*La maleta, El retorno, El tango del viudo*) como del primer largometraje ruiciano de 1968, *Tres tristes tigres* (inspirado en la obra teatral de Alejandro Sieveking, no en la novela homónima de Guillermo Cabrera Infante).

Los reseñistas antes mencionados subrayan el carácter erudito de la publicación. Dada la inevitable connotación aparejada a la idea "erudición," quisiéramos puntualizar. Este carácter surge tanto de su dimensión académica, como de la necesidad de una aproximación al nivel del carácter intelectual del cine de Ruiz. Nada más alejado del temple del libro que la disección fría y abstrusa que tal calificativo podría dar lugar a entender. Muy al contrario, *La tristeza de los tigres* revela un acercamiento afectivo al cine del autor que actúa como fuerza dinamizadora de una inquisición extremadamente rigurosa.

Podemos sintetizar las mayores aportaciones del libro en cuatro puntos esenciales: la recuperación del contexto histórico-cultural y biográfico del autor a finales de los años 60; la atención matizada, como nunca hasta la fecha, de las relaciones entre cine y literatura en el cine de Ruiz; el estudio de los principios éticos y estéticos que rigen la trayectoria continua y evolutiva del cineasta; y el deslumbrante análisis de la película *Tres tristes tigres.*

En primer lugar, la recuperación del marco contextual, en el que Ruiz y toda una generación de nuevos cineastas se formó a finales de los años 60, permite una comprensión mucho más cabal de los paradigmas en torno a los cuales nace su singularísima propuesta estética. Cortínez y Engelbert dirigen nuestra atención hacia el enclave histórico del 68 chileno (frecuentemente arrinconado debido a su coincidencia con hitos como la revolución estudiantil en Francia, la masacre de Tlatelolco o la primavera de Praga), al tiempo que integran los inicios de un cine joven en línea con una nueva sentimentalidad, promocionada desde el Estado y la crítica periodística. Los directores chilenos de este enclave histórico se inscriben en una encrucijada de renovación tanto a nivel nacional como a escala internacional. El cine de Ruiz, desde sus inicios, trata de aislarse de las tendencias en boga, tanto de las propuestas comerciales, a lo Germán Becker (*Ayúdeme Ud. compadre*), como del cine documental y de denuncia de directores como Álvaro Covacevich (*Morir un poco*), Patricio Kaulen (*Largo viaje*), Aldo Francia (*Valparaíso mi amor*) o Miguel Littin (*El chacal de Nahueltoro*). La fe en la indagación filosófica y experimental hará de Ruiz una *rara avis* desde sus comienzos, con su primer film proyectado en cines, *Tres tristes tigres* de 1968. Este recorrido en el plano nacional chileno tiene como aliciente añadido su imbricación en el contexto cinematográfico internacional. Todo conocedor del cine estadounidense agradecerá las correlaciones del cine de Ruiz con el de directores como Arthur Penn (*Bonny and Clyde*) o Mike Nichols (*The Graduate*).

La segunda gran aportación del volumen radica en la iluminadora atención a las relaciones entre cine y literatura, en particular el teatro, dentro de la obra ruiciana. En una producción tan claramente vinculada al arte literario (desde la reciente *Mistérios de Lisboa,* basada en una novela de Castelo Branco, hasta las libérrimas versiones fílmicas de *L'Île au tresor* sobre texto de Stevenson, *Le temps retrouvé* inspirada en Proust o *La vida es sueño* de Calderón) el análisis de esta relación resulta inevitable. Urgía, desde hacía algún tiempo, que las frecuentes simplificaciones sobre el sentido de ciertos textos y autores en su filmografía se vieran corregidas. Así, por ejemplo, Ruiz ha sido motejado frecuentemente de brechtiano o borgeano sin ningún tipo de matizaciones al respecto, sin atender, por encima de temas o procedimientos (el laberinto metafísico de Borges, la técnica de distanciamiento de Brecht), el uso e intención específicos de su cine. Cortínez y Engelbert marcan una pauta clara para distinguir hasta qué punto el director sigue a algunos de sus escritores predilectos, y en qué punto se aparta de ellos.

El análisis interdisciplinario entre cine y literatura abarca también los puntos de contacto entre los principios estéticos de autores como Ruiz y Cortázar. Estos pasajes no solo sirven a la comunicación de los valores fílmicos del director chileno para con el lector especialista en literatura, sino que permiten una inscripción de su cine en línea a grandes figuras de la cultura, un espacio, que lamentablemente, le ha sido arrebatado a Ruiz en demasiadas ocasiones.

Dentro de las relaciones entre cine y literatura, destaca la importancia de la significativa vinculación con el teatro. Recordemos que el director se forma como dramaturgo en sus comienzos, desde que en 1959 participa en el Centro Universitario de Teatro de la Universidad Federico Santa María en Valparaíso. No es hasta el descubrimiento de las limitaciones estéticas que el futuro cineasta encuentra en lo dramático, que se siente llamado a la exploración fílmica. Las primeras tentativas (de proyección frustrada) se mueven en el espacio del cortometraje y la inspiración teatral: *La maleta* y *El retorno*, ambos de 1963, sobre guiones del propio director. La propia inquietud del joven cineasta consigna al estancamiento y posterior abandono de ambos cortometrajes. Los proyectos sobre material literario se acumulan. Ruiz se interesa en adaptaciones libres de poemas de Pablo Neruda ("Tango del viudo"), Enrique Lihn ("Monólogo del profesor con su alumno") y Jorge Teillier ("Adiós muchacho"), de las cuales solo la primera encuentra traducción fílmica. Este corpus de trabajos ya adelanta la que será una fructífera relación interdisciplinaria (marcada con frecuencia, eso sí, por la subordinación del texto al poder de la imagen).

Como tercera de las aportaciones, cabría destacar la sistematización de las características de estilo del director. Cortínez y Engelbert profundizan no solo en el mensaje de filiación existencialista o en la práctica de narración de tendencia rizomática común a buena parte de su producción, sino que se adentran en el especializado campo de su sintaxis fílmica. El rescate de la teoría de los planos de Raúl Ruiz resulta una herramienta útil a la hora de comprender las preferencias del director por ciertas formas de filmación y edición, que sirven de correlato a sus preocupaciones filosóficas e intelectuales. En este contexto, es de notar la precisión con la cual las múltiples ilustraciones apoyan e iluminan el argumento analítico. Se puede pensar, por ejemplo, en la aparición del capitalista anónimo y su inserción en una red de planos a través de lo que Ruiz llama la "función centrífuga del plano" (209, 253, 266).

Por último, merece mención especial el detallado análisis de *Tres tristes tigres*. Sorprende el hecho de que, hasta la publicación de este libro, la crítica no haya profundizado en el valor de esta *opera prima*. Cortínez y Engelbert cubren con el capítulo dedicado al largometraje uno de los vacíos críticos más urgentes y necesarios. A lo largo de cien páginas, los autores completan un pormenorizado estudio, secuencia por secuencia, que constituye toda una lección magistral de cómo un texto cinematográfico ha de ser analizado. Con el capítulo final, ambos profesores cierran el arco de estudio abierto por los capítulos precedentes sobre el cine inicial hasta enlazarlo con su producción última, *Mistérios de Lisboa*, último largometraje estrenado en vida por Raúl Ruiz. La tesis central de este capítulo—que toda la producción cinematográfica de Ruiz obedecería a un mecanismo psicosocial de afirmación identitaria, un *habitus* en el sentido de Pierre Bourdieu (295-301)—es tan sugerente como provocadora. La validez de esta clave para los misterios de Raúl Ruiz espera su verificación o desmantelamiento a través de subsiguientes análisis de algunas de las películas que aún quedan por cubrir.

En conclusión, libro bastante recomendable no solo para los especialistas en el cine del director chileno o en el de su generación, sino también para aquellos que deseen penetrar en formas eficientes de análisis fílmico y en las intrincadas relaciones entre cine y literatura.

Juan Jesús Payán
University of California, Los Angeles

CABRERA, ANA MARÍA. *Felicitas Guerrero: "La mujer más hermosa de la República."* Buenos Aires: Emecé, 2012. 286 pp.

A catorce años de su primera publicación vuelve a editarse en versión escolar la novela *Felicitas Guerrero* de la profesora y escritora argentina Ana María Cabrera. La novela, que se convirtió rápidamente en *best-seller*, se ha impreso catorce veces. La presente edición cuenta con un breve prólogo de María Kodama, viuda del escritor Jorge Luis Borges.

Partiendo de un suceso verídico que ha permanecido en la memoria histórica en forma de leyenda, la autora elabora un texto literario donde explora las costumbres de la Argentina decimonónica y las restricciones que esas mismas prácticas imponían a las mujeres de la época. *Felicitas Guerrero* es una novela histórica que narra el asesinato en 1872 de una joven de alta sociedad a manos de un enamorado despechado. Siendo viuda, rica y hermosa, Felicitas se convierte en la obsesión de Enrique Ocampo, quien no puede tolerar que la joven se haya enamorado de otro hombre. Pese a ser este el suceso que da pie a la trama, la novela se abre con una crónica social de tono machista donde se transfiere la responsabilidad por la muerte de Felicitas a la coquetería femenina. Mediante la incorporación de un fragmento de la crónica, la autora sienta la pauta del contenido feminista que subyace en la novela y que se opone a la ideología que predominaba en la sociedad del siglo XIX. La narración se encarga posteriormente de descartar la perspectiva masculina al develar la historia de una mujer que lucha constantemente por hacerse de un espacio propio en una época en que le estaba vedado valerse por sí misma y amar libremente.

Con evidente conocimiento de la crítica feminista contemporánea, Cabrera destaca temas tan importantes como el matrimonio, el trabajo, la sexualidad, la violencia contra la mujer, la escritura femenina y las disposiciones jurídicas que garantizan su estado de dependencia. La autora aprovecha asimismo la coyuntura que presenta el momento histórico que abarca la vida de Felicitas para vincular el desarrollo de la nueva conciencia feminista con la consolidación de la nación argentina. Referencias al ambiente político y económico, a figuras históricas de importancia, a la ideología positivista que predominaba en el pensamiento del periodo; así como la inserción de textos literarios claves en la construcción de la identidad nacional—como el *Martín Fierro*—y la inclusión de personajes como el jurista Cristián

Demaría—defensor de los derechos de la mujer—contribuyen al enlazamiento de lo femenino con lo nacional. De igual manera, la incorporación de fragmentos de poemas, crónicas de la época y de trozos del propio diario de Felicitas hace de la novela un texto útil para iniciar a los alumnos en los estudios literarios.

La nueva edición escolar de *Felicitas Guerrero* provee al lector de una sección con actividades para el análisis de la lectura y un manual de propuestas metodológicas para el docente. La guía de comprensión de lectura contiene ejercicios para el estudio detallado de los aspectos literarios, históricos y temáticos que se advierten en los diferentes capítulos. Por su parte, el manual para el docente tiene como uno de sus propósitos proporcionar la teoría necesaria para exponer las tendencias literarias que influyen en la elaboración del texto a los estudiantes. La inclusión de herramientas que facilitan el esclarecimiento del contexto histórico y teórico es precisamente uno de los méritos de la nueva edición de *Felicitas Guerrero*. Otorga un valor adicional a esta publicación la reproducción como parte de los materiales complementarios de un relato de la escritora Juana Manuela Gorriti sobre los mismos hechos. El cuento "Feliza" de Gorriti no solamente brinda la perspectiva de una de las escritoras más destacadas del siglo XIX, sino que permite que los estudiantes realicen una comparación entre ambos textos.

En términos generales la minuciosa investigación llevada a cabo por Cabrera enriquece la historia de Felicitas hasta convertirla en una novela que abarca temas transcendentales para la literatura feminista. *Felicitas Guerrero* es, tanto en su forma como en su contenido, una novela que pudo haber sido escrita en el siglo XIX pero que tuvo que esperar 126 años para ser rescatada de entre las cenizas de la leyenda popular.

Brenda Ortiz-Loyola
University of California, Los Angeles

www.ingramcontent.com/pod-product-compliance
Lightning Source LLC
Chambersburg PA
CBHW060404030726
47497CB00003B/840